About the Author

MICHAEL SIMMONS was educated at St Paul's School and Emmanuel College, Cambridge. He is a retired lawyer who practised in Central London and the City for over 50 years. He also had a part-time career as a legal journalist, lecturer, writer and consultant in professional services management and marketing. He is the author of *Low Life Lawyer* and the *Lawyer Who Couldn't Sit Still*; also published by Book Guild as well as other books. He and his wife live in London.

www.michaelsimmonsauthor.com

To Jo

Double Exposure

Michael Simmons

The Book Guild Ltd

First published in Great Britain in 2018 by
The Book Guild Ltd
9 Priory Business Park
Wistow Road, Kibworth
Leicestershire, LE8 0RX
Freephone: 0800 999 2982
www.bookguild.co.uk
Email: info@bookguild.co.uk
Twitter: @bookguild

This work is entirely fictitious and bears no resemblance to any persons living or dead.

Typeset in Adobe Garamond Pro

Printed and bound in Great Britain by CPI Group (UK) Ltd, Croydon, CR0 4YY

ISBN 9781912362 530

British Library Cataloguing in Publication Data.
A catalogue record for this book is available from the British Library.

To Harry and Ella.
Your time will come

ACKNOWLEDGMENTS

Whatever they tell you, it is impossible to write a book like this without help. Others are needed if only to provide a sense of perspective. Mine and a lot more came from my wife, Samantha, my son, Edward, and once again from my old school friend, Mark Lovell and eagle-eyed Tom Osborne.

I owe a lot to everyone at my publishers, Book Guild, who throughout radiated cheerful competence and encouragement and I must not forget all the support I received from Daunts Books at Holland Park.

Once again, please don't look for real people and events in the pages of this book. I made it all up!

1

In a Mist

Sophie

I tried to see out from the kitchen window but swirling clouds cut us off from the rest of the world. The silence was complete. It felt as if we were lost in outer space. I had taken the children out in it earlier in the day but we speedily returned to the comfort of our centrally heated house. Luckily, it wasn't a school day. It was not only extremely cold but exceedingly wet. Globules of water quickly formed on our exposed skin. We had to imagine the buildings around us and those few remaining inhabitants huddled together to retain warmth and sanity. Now that it was dark as well, it was even spookier.

It had not been like that when we arrived, tired and hungry, in mid-October just a few months ago when the sun had been shining brightly in a clear sky. The trattoria was snug and warm and we were made very welcome. Rodolfo, the owner, was obviously very practised with foreigners of all descriptions and was not put out by the arrival of a dishevelled, middle-aged Englishwoman with two small children in tow. After fragrant bowls of *acquacotta*, the local bread soup, and veal cutlets cooked to perfection, I relaxed over an espresso while the children raided the ice cream cabinet.

1

I think that Rodolfo was surprised by my relative fluency in Italian. I know I was surprised too at how easily it came back. A combination of cheap family holidays, school trips, serving at table in the local spaghetti joint at home and a succession of unsuitable Italian boyfriends in Oxford had given me a head start. We had been running away for many months and the initial panic had subsided. I felt that now was the time to stop and reconsider our lives. This was as good a place as any to do it.

By now, the other customers had slipped away and I could hear the sound of shutters going up and shops reopening after their lengthy midday break. I had noticed a rather smart-looking estate agency just a few doors up on the way in. I paid Rodolfo's very reasonable bill and took the children into the agency.

Enrico was very smooth and seemed hungry for my business. I explained that I was a writer who wanted six months' solitude and seclusion to complete my project. The children could go to the local junior school. Enrico pulled a number of sets of keys from a board and we started climbing into the old village through the narrow, medieval-looking archway. I felt we were going back into ancient times as the grey stone walls rapidly closed in around us.

I found what I wanted right at the top of the village. The house looked as if it was built into the rock itself and constructed of the local grey stone, with brown wooden shutters. It was much too big but I loved the ancient square and the prime position that the house occupied as one whole side of it. In my mind we were still running away and this location gave us the opportunity for an early sighting of any pursuers. The views overall were amazing. I stood entranced on the back terrace, alternately gazing at the islands of Giglio and Elba and the sea in between, shining silver in the late afternoon sun while the children climbed shrieking up and down the rocks. It was a very clear day and I could see cars moving and the static plumes of smoke from farmers' fires on the seemingly flat plain below. This village was built to withstand a siege. I thought of the inhabitants hundreds of years ago spotting the coming of a marauding band of Moorish pirates down below, rushing to collect their livestock grazing in the fields, herding them into the village square, bolting the gates and preparing to meet the coming onslaught. I did not want to dwell too much on the parallels of our current situation.

The asking rent was ridiculously low, and after some hard bargaining, even less. We returned to Enrico's office to sign the papers and it did not take us long to transfer our few suitcases from the rented car parked below to our new home. Travelling on easyJet to Pisa does not encourage you to bring loads of luggage. The house was fully equipped but I knew that in the next few days we could work out what we lacked and buy it in the village or the nearby town of Grosseto. The children rushed from room to room, staking their claim to beds in the most unsuitable places. I needed them near me for the inevitable moment when they woke up terrified in the middle of the night in unfamiliar surroundings. As it was, I was worried how I was going to get them to sleep at their current levels of excitement, but I need not have been concerned. They were fast asleep as soon as their heads touched the pillows. It had been a long day.

What I liked was that there were hardly any neighbours. It was different in the summer, I was assured, when all the holiday home owners returned with the accompanying tourists but now there was only the widow, Rosetta, and her dog, Bricola, to keep us company. All the other houses were boarded up for the season with their brown or green shutters tightly closed. The lime tree in the middle of the square had shed its leaves for the winter and, strangely enough, the very air of desolation and desertion served to raise my spirits. I had had enough of towns and big cities for the time being. The words of the Latin poet Horace came back to me: *Odi profanum vulgus et arceo*. 'I hate the common herd and avoid it' is about the best translation I can find.

While the children were at school, I loved to wander around the narrow streets and alleys. I discovered a talent for sketching that I never knew I had. I concentrated particularly on the doorways and windows. Some looked as if they had not received a coat of paint for centuries. I even found a Byzantine window that could have been from another country in another age. There were bridges and dark tunnels leading nowhere. An unsightly pile of builders' debris sat next to a carefully tended wooden tub of bright red geraniums. Alleyways with no apparent purpose abounded and I got the impression that the whole place was thrown together higgledy-piggledy. Although piped methane gas had been brought to the village, there was still the pungent smell of woodsmoke to delight my nostrils. Such inhabitants as there were greeted my activities with a tolerant smile. They were uniformly elderly and looked as weathered and gnarled as the buildings themselves.

I was concerned that the children would find it difficult to adjust to the loss, or at least the absence, of their parents; the ubiquitous presence of me, their aunt and not least Italian village life but I need not have worried too much. Charlotte looked very much like her mother and me: tall for her age with dark hair and long, slender limbs, still growing fast and in spurts but likely at some stage to fill out. She particularly loved her new school and the relaxed way of teaching. There seemed to be no language barrier for her and she brought home a constant stream of new friends and correspondingly was always being entertained in other homes. There were far too many times when she was not able to eat the supper that I had prepared as she had been stuffed with cake and biscuits in the kitchens of her classmates' parents after school. Her Italian was becoming so good and colloquial that I sometimes found it difficult to follow her conversation. Of course she missed her parents. I had managed to salvage, at the last minute before our precipitate departure, a photo of both of them and I had this copied and framed in the town so that they both had it by their bedsides. Loving child that she was, Charlotte kept hers bordered with wild flowers and grasses. I made sure that we talked about them a lot.

Ivan in appearance was nothing like either of his parents or me: small, ginger, freckled and wiry, he seemed to be in perpetual motion. He found it far harder to fit into the new environment. He was clearly missing his father particularly. I had rather fudged the issue of Igor's death with him out of a desire to protect him and not face the truth. He still sometimes thought that Daddy was going to come back. Sooner or later I was going to have to tell him for certain that he was dead. I made sure that we talked about Hannah, my identical twin sister, and Igor as much as possible, though I felt that there was little chance that Ivan would forget them. His memories of them remained recent and vivid. Temperamentally, by contrast and as something of a paradox in relation to his physical behaviour, he was withdrawn and thoughtful, rather like his father. I felt that he needed more time to accept our new life. I sat down with him every afternoon after school with an Italian reading book. He was improving slowly but it was doing wonders for my own language skills. Fortunately, there were a couple of boys from the village who clearly liked him and noisy games of football in the square outside were becoming more frequent.

An unexpected visit from the carabinieri broke the pattern of our days. The *brigadiere* or sergeant was flanked by two troopers carrying well-oiled and businesslike sub-machine guns. He came to introduce himself and warn me of the dangers that a woman alone in this village faced from predatory men. At the same time, by the way he was hungrily looking me up and down, I felt that the greatest threat to my person came from the man directly in front of me. He could have been quite attractive but for the large khaki-clad gut overhanging his well-polished belt. He left with the message that he and his men were there to protect me and handed me a card with his office telephone number and the statement that I could call any time. Late one Saturday night when a group of drunken youths gathered outside the house and refused to move when I asked them as I was worried that they would wake the children, I did telephone only to be greeted by an answerphone message that the office was closed and I should call again after nine the next morning. So much for round-the-clock protection.

Now, as I looked out at the swirling fog-like cloud, I could have wished for more people around. But was it as silent outside as I had thought? I could definitely hear footsteps trudging cautiously round the house. It sounded like a group of rather large men and they were making no real attempt to move quietly. Suddenly, I heard the sound of the handle on the back terrace door being cautiously turned. They had caught up with us! I grabbed the children and we rushed to hide in the cubbyhole under the stairs that I had previously designated as our bolthole in an emergency such as this. I had thought it unlikely that they would track us down, but how wrong I was.

There was a splintering crash of breaking wood which I recognised as the shuttered door leading to the rear terrace, followed immediately by smashing glass as they attacked the door behind it. They were now in the house. There was the sound of heavy boots as their owners cautiously explored the empty rooms in the dark or perhaps with the aid of a flashlight. I was too busy keeping the children's heads down as close to me as possible to look up to see. We cowered in terror. I knew it was only a question of time before we were discovered and dragged out to await our fate. I expected no mercy for myself but what would they do to the children?

As these thoughts were going round in my head, there was the booming sound of an explosion at the front door and the rush of still more heavy feet. There were numerous popping sounds and our confined space quickly filled with acrid smoke which stung our eyes, together with the stench of cordite. I recognised from the movies the sounds of silenced gunfire but I could not understand the accompanying shouts in neither Italian nor English. All that activity seemed to be over in a flash and once again was followed by complete silence.

Rough hands suddenly grabbed us and we stood, trembling and blinking, in the strong light of torches shone directly in our eyes. It seemed to take endless time before I could focus but, when I could, I was not encouraged by what I saw. There were three men facing us, dressed from head to foot in black. The two tattooed gorillas on either side like bookends were enormous. The one in the middle was not smiling. We had never met but it was somehow inevitable that he would be our immediate rescuer, one of the biggest Russian oligarchs of them all, whose photograph appeared often in the British media. What was his long-term game plan for us? He owed me no favours but I hoped that he would spare the children.

Out of the corner of my eye, I noticed five newly-wrapped, large cylindrical bundles by a wall, and put myself in a position to try to prevent the children seeing them. The silence seemed endless as the man in the middle examined the three of us closely. I had far too much time to think. How on earth had I got myself, my young niece and even younger nephew into this life-threatening situation? As a respectable and successful female City solicitor, the worst thing likely to have happened to me before now was being 'felt up' in a crowded underground train in the rush hour, unless I went off the rails professionally, which was down to me alone. I had merely stepped of necessity into an existing drama following the horrible and untimely deaths of my twin sister Hannah and her husband, Igor, without having the slightest idea of what I was involving myself in. Was Hannah to blame and could I have avoided being caught up in this terrifying series of events?

Hannah had also been a solicitor but practising in the London suburbs with the chain of office of the presidency of her local law society after thirty years of devoted service as the acme of her expectations in life. How had she got us all into this ghastly mess? I put it down to a mixture of ambition, naivety and despair, all utterly pardonable in the particular circumstances where I, so closely linked as we were, had blindly to follow. Were the five cylindrical bundles about to be increased by three more? If Hannah and I had not been identical twins, would there even have been a tale to be told at all? This is our story, which both of us need to tell.

2

Sisters

Hannah

Unless you are an identical twin yourself, you have no idea how much it sets you apart from other people. Produced as you are from the same egg, you have so much more affinity than fraternal twins, who are born from separate eggs and are often of different sexes. Identical twins are always of the same sex. The two of you seem to look out at the world with one pair of eyes. The enemy of one is the enemy of both. There is much less need for outside friendships as your twin is your very best friend. In fact, if one twin seeks to make an outside friendship, the other is likely to become insanely jealous and do her best to destroy the new relationship. Twins are often slow to develop normal communication skills as they are bound up with each other and have less need than ordinary people for verbal communication, as instinct and intuition are so strong between them. They seem to have their own language. While they are united against the outside world, this does not mean that the relationship between twins is harmonious – quite the reverse. Their quarrels and arguments are far more serious and deeply felt, though they are usually quick to reconcile but not always. They can fight like wildcats. Theirs is a true love/hate relationship.

I have no doubt that there was a telepathic understanding between us. I discussed this with Sophie and she agreed. It did not matter how far apart we were physically; if one of us was in need, it was as though an alarm bell went off in the other's head. Several times when I was in trouble, Sophie came unexpectedly to my rescue. "I just knew you needed me," was her invariable response when I asked her why she was there. I did the same for her as many times. The classic occasion was in adolescence when Sophie had gone off to see *La Ronde* in an outlying cinema in Oxford with a young don whom she fancied madly. I had cycled into town for a drink on my own at a seedy pub which was forbidden to undergraduates in the hope of meeting a man, a bit of rough trade, whom I was targeting at the time. He was not there but I was ambushed in a dark passage on the way to the ladies' by three drunk labourers who clearly meant me harm. I was doing my best to sweet-talk them but they were steadily pushing me into a corner, beginning to mess around with my clothes and touching me all over.

Sophie

I was enjoying the twists and turns of the film and also Ed's warm hand on my thigh, when I suddenly knew I should not be there and that Hannah needed me urgently. It was as though an explosion had gone off in my brain. I could not sit there a moment longer. I made a perfunctory apology to Ed and dashed out. Fortunately, I had left my bike right outside and I pedalled madly to the pub where I knew I would find Hannah. She was not in the bar but I found her at the end of the passage past the ladies'. One of the gang had his hand over her mouth to stop her screaming and another had hoisted her legs over his shoulders. I yelled at the top of my voice and pitched in with clawed fingers aimed at their eyes and my feet and knees at their balls. Surprise was everything and they dashed off as quickly as they could, leaving me to comfort a very shaken Hannah.

"You really knew I needed you," She said to me as she recovered.

"Yes, it was as if I felt your distress as a cry for help from within my innermost being," I replied.

Hannah

Sophie and I were born six minutes apart. She was the older and regularly behaved as such. The difference might as well have been six years. I almost always slipped into the role of the feckless and irresponsible younger sister, while she took responsibility and played the leader when she was in the mood. Our mother alone could tell us apart and only after some thought. This gave us ample scope for crafty substitutions, particularly to escape punishment for our sins. The one would slip readily into the other's place with loud protestations of innocence. By the time the perpetrator was found, it was often too late for punishment. The fact that we dressed identically and wore our hair in the same style merely reinforced the deception. I can see now that there was a lot of cruelty in our behaviour to others. We were big for our age and far more intelligent than the village boys and girls and showed them no mercy. We were good fighters too and often left those unwise enough to tangle with us bruised and bleeding. If you took on one of us, you found yourself having to fight both. We became bored far too easily and hence drifted into delinquency.

We were born and brought up in a village a cycle ride from Oxford. Father was the local vicar and Mother was the librarian for one of the more obscure Anglican foundations in the city. Our arrival caught everybody by surprise. The doctor thought that Mother was merely carrying one very large baby, her first and last. We were so placed in the womb, one behind the other, that his stethoscope did not pick up our separate heart beats. As a result, no plans were made for my arrival and that state of confusion seemed to affect both of us (especially me) throughout our childhood and early adolescence. Our very existence was something of an embarrassment to our parents. In an ideal world, we would have been kept apart in the west wing with numerous nannies and governesses and merely brought out to be displayed favourably on special occasions. Unfortunately, the genteel poverty of our father's calling and our mother's profession pushed us all potentially into far too much proximity. We knew that we were not wanted, so we spent as much time out of the house as possible. The village itself was far too constricting. The truth was that this village or any village for that matter, was too small to contain us. We were continually getting into trouble.

As Father was always seemingly locked away in his study writing his Sunday sermon and Mother was in Oxford doing whatever librarians do or cycling back and forth between home and college, we were brought up by Mrs Higgs, the local 'treasure'. She was so busy playing the part of the treasure that nobody except Sophie and I understood how thoroughly lazy and corrupt she really was. As a result, we ran wild.

Mrs Higgs

I would not say that the twins were evil but they certainly had a spiteful streak in them. You made a mistake if you judged them on their looks alone. They were tall for their age, well built with manes of dark hair and by general agreement very beautiful. They had a Spanish look about them. They usually looked like angels but they could behave like devils. You crossed either or both of them at your peril. I got no support from their mother or father if I complained or tried to discipline them, so I found it best to take the easy way out. If they got into trouble, I'd let their parents or teachers sort it out. As it was, they got away with murder. 'Cunning' was not the word for it. I viewed my job as looking after the house, cooking for the twins and clearing up their mess. It was always a relief when Mrs Hoare got home and I could leave for the day. If a day passed without something dreadful happening on my watch, I thought of myself as lucky. *Heaven help the men they marry*, I used to think, though I doubted whether any decent men would have them.

Hannah

We only lasted one term at the local primary school before our parents were informed that we were such a bad influence that the head teacher was threatening to resign, with the attendant risk of the school closing down. It was suggested that one of us should stay while the other went to school in Oxford itself. Our combined objections were so strong that this idea was quickly dropped and we were both sent off to the private school in the city best known for its academic rigour and discipline. We responded well to the former and battled constantly against the latter element. The school took children all the way through to eighteen, and though feeble attempts were made to move us on, we resisted and found ourselves ultimately as joint head girls with open major scholarships to different colleges in Cambridge.

Margaret Livesey

I knew I was buying trouble when I agreed to take on the twins. They had wrecked their little school in Wheatley to the point that the head teacher had a choice of closure or suicide. I was much more arrogant and energetic in those days though and I reckoned that I could handle the dual problem. I ultimately did but there were many sticky moments in their time with us. I was once visited by the manager of the largest record shop in Oxford, accompanied by two policemen. The shop had been experiencing an extraordinary number of thefts of stock on display. Somehow the twins were always there or thereabouts, though nothing yet could be proved against them. The most audacious episode involved the placing of the manager's jacket ten feet high over the lens of a tracking CCTV camera so the identity of the thief could be concealed. I was asked if I could help by making the shop out of bounds but I was fairly sure that whatever I did would be ineffective. I was experienced with disruptive pupils but not with disruptive twins where one plus one seemed always to make three. The only way to handle them was to keep them busy. They absorbed knowledge like blotting paper and one challenge lay in keeping them from getting so far ahead that the other girls got discouraged.

I turned a blind eye as much as possible to their extracurricular activities. I was concerned that they would lead other girls into their unsavoury sexual exploits but here the twin element worked to our advantage as they hunted as a pair to the exclusion of all others. There were some very dark episodes along the way and I spent more time and effort in diplomatic handling of the twins and those complaining about them than on the rest of the school combined. The results at the end of the day were there to see. I made them joint head girls, to a chorus of disapproval from the rest of the staff. It turned out to be an inspired appointment. Apart from their irritating habit of viewing themselves as shop stewards for the trade union of girls against their bosses, the teachers, they did an excellent job.

As to the next step, Oxford was obviously out. They were too well known in the colleges already, for all the wrong reasons. To attend as students would mean three years of anticlimax – if they managed to last that long. A fast stream of quasi-criminality flowed just beneath the surface in both of them and the risk would be too great. It had to be Cambridge, where the seventy-mile gap was sufficiently wide to ensure that their reputations had not preceded them. By then, I had no doubt that they would achieve top scholarships for entry. I was not disappointed.

Hannah

It was a single-sex school but that did nothing to hinder our sexual development and experimentation. As the older sister, Sophie quite properly lost her virginity first as part of an operation which we had jointly planned. The chosen instrument of our serial deflowering was the son of the local lord of the manor, during his holiday before his last term at Eton prior to three years at Christ Church. He was, at least in our eyes, a mature eighteen, while we were fast approaching fifteen, although our physical maturity was racing crazily ahead. The chosen venue was Shotover Hill, a well-known local beauty spot and lovers' lane, while the site was the commodious back seat of his father's vintage Bentley tourer. The odour of seasoned leather always had a special place in our sexual history ever after.

Sophie reported back to me on the encounter in a very matter-of-fact way, rather like a subaltern reporting to his company commander after a minor exercise in no-man's-land. Three days later, it was my turn. We reckoned that would give him sufficient recovery time and I duly presented myself, dressed identically and doused in the same perfume from our mother's dressing table. He assumed that he was getting a second bite of the same cherry and had no idea that I was someone other than Sophie. This was typical of the games we played and it was rather cruel to deprive him of the opportunity of boasting that he had taken the virginity of both of the beautiful but infamous Hoare twins in quick succession. Physically, the loss of our virginity was no big deal. Our active lifestyle coupled with personal and mutual exploration provided us with some disappointment. We had read all that stuff about blood on the sheets but in our case there was not one spot on the well-worn leather of the vast and thickly-padded back seat of the car and you may be sure that we gave it a thorough examination with a torch, completely ignoring the questions with which the Honourable Nigel was bombarding us. Having fulfilled his duty, we no longer had any interest in him. As for the expected pain, we experienced none at all and were merely left wondering why we had waited so long and what all the fuss was about. There was certainly a lot more to come in that department for both of us.

For the rest of our time at school, we did our best to live up to our surname. We were a common sight, cycling madly from assignation to assignation with our cloaks flying behind us in the wind as we pedalled at maximum speed. We quickly ran through the undergraduate ranks, created havoc among the postgraduates and scandal in the households of numerous lecherous younger married dons. While we concentrated on the 'gown' element of Oxford, we did not entirely neglect the 'town'. We were more than familiar with all the low places where undergraduates were discouraged if not actually forbidden from visiting. Our choice of men ranged from the unsuitable to the unspeakable.

We had outworn our welcome in Oxford and scholarships to Cambridge gave us the opportunity to make a fresh start. It was not a decision that was reached easily. For once, I was the leader. Frankly, I was fed up with always being in the shadow of my older twin sister. I felt that I was regarded as having no personality or identity of my own, a mere clone of Sophie. We had a blazing row about it when I raised the subject. Sophie could not see what my problem was and why I was making such a fuss about it. She was perfectly content with the current situation. The argument went on for weeks before she saw my side of it. To her credit, once she did she accepted that there had to be a new start made so that we could develop as two separate personalities rather than as two sides of the same coin. After the decision had been made, we talked it through carefully. Accordingly, I started at a co-educational college while Sophie chose the monastic seclusion of a single-sex one. This was our attempt at an early divorce. We each needed to start being known as individuals rather than as one of a pair, rather like candlesticks.

If we were to develop separate personalities, we had to start by ceasing to dress and look alike. I visited the hairdresser and came back with a short but tightly curled perm. Sophie opted for a continuation of her long, flowing locks, although she did experiment with putting them up in a pleat or bun. I went for the jeans-and-voluminous-sweater look. Sophie by contrast was influenced by the flower power movement and dressed in a floaty, diaphanous style with massive ropes of ethnic jewellery around her neck and wrists. Unless you concentrated hard, you would no longer know that we were identical twins.

3

Varsity Drag

Professor Augusta Sinclair

Sophie Hoare was one of the best students I have ever had. I have always reckoned that academic law is for the few and that most use it solely as a means to an end towards professional qualification and a subsequent legal career either at the Bar or as a solicitor. Sophie by contrast was a natural and analytical academic. I worried that she did not seek the delights of Cambridge like so many students but was bound up in her studies. She came across as rather world-wear, as if she had seen it all before. I spent the last six months of her time as an undergraduate preparing a niche for her to combine postgraduate research with sufficient paid teaching to keep body and soul together. Imagine my shock and disappointment when, having collected her anticipated starred first, she announced that she was going to qualify as a solicitor and pursue a career in one of the large City law firms.

She did soften the blow slightly by agreeing to take on some part-time supervision of second and third year contract law students, as well as doing an external master's degree under my tutelage but it was not the same thing.

Sophie

Cambridge for me was something of a three-year hiatus or anticlimax. I suppose we were completely spoiled by the social life that we had enjoyed in Oxford. From before the age of fifteen we had been living as undergraduates by night and schoolchildren by day. Cambridge had nothing to offer me on the former front. I had seen and done it all. However, entering the academic world was for me like entering an Aladdin's cave. Here was my chance to catch up and bring my life into balance. I ignored all social invitations: been there, done that. Sex was a bit of a problem: I was used to so much of it and so often. However, I was sick of the routine posturing required to get to the point of satisfaction and as to the aftermath… I therefore largely relied on me to pleasure myself with the assistance of what I called my 'pocket rocket'. If the urge occasionally did get too much, I would dress like a tart in a tight, low-cut blouse and short, split skirt with an old raincoat over the top until I was out of sight of the college. Before I went into action, I would visit the ladies' room, make myself up to look the part and smother myself in liberal doses of cheap perfume. I targeted one or other of the rather notorious and seedy pubs in the town where it was easy to pick up some rough trade for the night without any comeback or awkward questions asked. It was always strictly at his place and never at mine. I suppose I was lucky but I never got into any trouble. I was a bit too big to be easily intimidated and looked as if I knew how to handle myself.

Poor Augusta, I think she rather fancied me in her dried-up way. Apart from some early experimentation and role play with Hannah, I had never gone in for that side of things. I did feel bad about letting her down on the academic front. She had lobbied so hard on my behalf with the faculty, who seemed suspicious of me but after the arid atmosphere of three years of academic law, I was ready for the raw meat of private practice. With my first-class degree, I had no difficulty landing a well-paid training contract with one of the top City firms. I had prepared the ground with a couple of vacation placements there when I had worked my socks off. They liked what they saw.

I did agree something of a compromise with Augusta. I would take the train up to Cambridge on Friday night, have a room in the college, dine in the hall with the other postgraduates and give a couple of supervisions on contract law to small groups of second and third-year law students on Saturday morning. The rest of the day was free for me to work in the library on the dissertation that I had agreed to write on the impact of Private International Law on certain aspects of commercial contracts. As a subject it sounded as dry as dust but it had a practical application and was carefully chosen to increase my usefulness with the firm, as well as my marketability if I moved on after qualifying. The firm also liked the idea of my Cambridge supervisions and I got quite a lot of kudos as a result. There was also time for some work with Augusta on the progress of my research and I timed my postgraduate degree exactly to coincide with the period of my training contract over two years.

I either returned to London on Saturday night or increasingly followed the urge to stay over. There was informal dining in the college at weekends and I would have something quickly from the buffet. I would then go back to my room and change into what I called my hunting gear. It was easy to slip out of a side door and make my way into town. There were a couple of men in different pubs whom I had trained to make love to me in ways that gave me maximum satisfaction. They knew not to ask me any questions. I was the cat who came and went as I pleased. In return, I gave them a far better time than they would get from any casual pick-up. I never stayed the night with them but would return to my room when I was ready. The college porters were discreet and turned a blind eye to my erratic schedule. I would sleep in on Sunday morning and return to London when I was ready.

The original question was whether Hannah was going to share a flat with me in London but this was now an academic proposition only. We had gone from the sublime to the ridiculous: from Oxford where we had lived in each other's pockets, to Cambridge where we had barely communicated at all and had somehow even managed to spend the vacations apart. Still, I missed my best friend and alter ego. I can't say that I approved of what I saw as her lack of ambition and being prepared to settle for second best. I had to accept that although identical twins, we were temperamentally entirely different. It was stupid of me at the time but I let my disappointment with Hannah show and this contributed to the deepening rift between us.

Hannah

It wasn't an easy decision but it was the best one, I'm sure. We were not Siamese twins and we had to get used to the idea of living our lives apart. We could always look back on those wonderful Oxford years when we had made a fool of the world but the time had come to do something different. We both agreed that we were tired of our man-eating ways. They were not men but merely boys. In fact we were fed up with that life altogether. School had been far too easy for us. We had collected our university scholarships like picking blackberries off a bush. Sophie wanted a life of academic rigour. I was almost ashamed to tell her but I wanted to settle down. A normal life with a husband and kids seemed very attractive after all we had been through in such a short space of time. I fancied waking up in the morning with the warmth and familiarity of one man's body next to me, though I had not met the right one yet. Meanwhile, I would take a degree in law and see what transpired.

Dr Ted Hardcastle

Hannah Hoare was not a special student and did nothing to stand out from the crowd except by her looks. Tall and imposing with curly dark hair, she made the other women seem like dwarves and some of the men too. I often felt that she was holding a lot back and could do so much better academically with her major scholarship. She came across as far more worldly and sophisticated than the rest of the class but she wasn't giving much away. There's always a lot of pairing off in the first year and it was no great surprise to hear that she had moved in with a Russian postgraduate law student, Igor Zabrinski, who was over from St Petersburg on a three-year doctoral programme.

Sophie

Of course, I had to know about Igor. Most of the time I resisted the temptation to make fun of Hannah in her broody phase, as I called it, but the 'divorce' between us was increasingly real. She brought him round to tea in my room and frankly he made no great impression on me. I resented the time that I had taken out from writing an important essay. Black, woolly sweater surmounted by a black, woolly beard and hair, coupled with a thick Russian accent and halting English, created quite a barrier between us and made intelligent conversation difficult if not impossible. He was being put on show for my approval, but I felt that if he was what Hannah wanted, she was welcome to him. I upset her a lot when we next met and she asked me what I thought about Igor. I told her that she could do a lot better and was wasting her opportunities. It was a real 'older sister' lecture. We did not speak to each other for some time after.

Hannah

I tried dating a few of the students in the faculty but it felt like Oxford all over again. I had just about resolved to spend the rest of my first term as a nun when I met Igor at a faculty drinks party. I nearly didn't go at all but I had missed the last two and felt that I needed to show solidarity and that I was a team player after all. He was sitting in a corner when I arrived rather late and the only available space to perch was on the arm of his chair. He was lonely and homesick but his little-boy-lost appeal sent flutters to the pit of my stomach. Replete with three cups of coffee, I dragged him back to my room and made slow, languorous love to him. His response was a lot better than his conversation. At least he was as tall as me. I was fed up with towering over men or wearing flat shoes so as not to inflate their inferiority complexes. I moved into his digs in Grantchester at the beginning of the next term and his English gradually improved. I made no effort to learn Russian.

Planning our life together after Cambridge took up much of our time. As my husband, he could stay in England and make a living through his Slav contacts. He did not want to qualify as a lawyer but preferred the life of a wheeler-dealer. I by contrast was determined to qualify as a solicitor and run my own practice as soon as I was allowed. He would supply me, so he said, with an inexhaustible supply of clients. In the absence of a better offer, it seemed good. I liked living with Igor despite his moods. He was great in bed and the give and take there somehow epitomised our relationship.

Igor abandoned his thesis halfway through and I managed to scrape an upper second in my finals. The next job was to find me a training contract with a small law firm in London with principals who would be susceptible to our ultimate takeover. We were true cuckoos in the nest. Igor offered a ready supply of clients and needed a commission-based consultancy. We were on offer as a package deal.

After a great deal of trial and error, the Appointments Board came up with just the job: a father-and-son practice in Ealing where the father was nearing retirement and the son was more enthusiastic about cultivating his allotment than wasting time in the office on legal matters and clients, though they both still needed an income to maintain their respective lifestyles. I missed not being able to talk it through with Sophie but we had had a steaming row over my relationship with Igor and were not speaking to each other.

Igor

I was a stranger in a strange land. The scholarship to do postgraduate work at Cambridge was something I nearly turned down. I was no extrovert and I did not know how I would handle such a different life. The more novels I read about life at Oxbridge, the more depressed I became. By the time I arrived I was not in the mood to assimilate at all. What I saw confirmed my prejudices. I did not want to float on a sea of sherry parties. I was seriously considering giving up and returning to Russia when I met Hannah. That such a beautiful and sophisticated woman was clearly interested in me made me feel alive again for the first time since I arrived in England. I had had girlfriends before but none who took the initiative and made love to me so wholeheartedly and with such abandon. I could not fail to respond and we embarked on a voyage of extreme sensuality that removed all my fears and doubts about life in England. I was totally absorbed in Hannah. In her arms, I could forget all my anxieties and sense of displacement.

My thesis was becoming increasingly pointless and irrelevant to me, so I gave it up. I could not spend my life in bed as Hannah's lover, though I was greatly tempted. She wanted a career as a lawyer but I was not interested myself, though I wanted to be around her and help her as much as possible. Although I was not naturally gregarious, I knew that I could easily become part of the expatriate Russian circles in London and steer their members to Hannah for legal work. It was not the career that I would naturally have chosen for myself but I was madly in love with Hannah and wanted to be near her and please her all the time. So we made our plans for the future together.

4

Strangers in the Night

Sophie

There was no question of Hannah and me sharing a flat after all. We were not communicating. I did feel a bit jealous that she was so much into Igor and so little now into me. We had tried going out as a threesome a couple of times but frankly I found Igor boring. All his Slavic brooding left me cold. He might be a great conversationalist in his original language but his English was just not up to it. Hannah and I eventually did make up but it was not the same as before. She and Igor found themselves a rather squalid flat in deepest Acton. In our earlier lives together, Hannah and I had been desperately untidy and relied on Mrs Higgs to follow us around and put everything back in order. After three years on my own in Cambridge, I had changed completely and now kept my home neat and tidy as I wanted it to be. Hannah had not changed at all and found a soulmate in Igor. Their place was an absolute stinking tip. I had to bite my tongue not to tell her so.

I wanted to conserve all my energies for work, so I rented a bedsitter in a flat in the Barbican about five minutes' brisk walk from the office. I reduced my physical possessions to the bare minimum apart from my large-screen computer and my small-screen television. There would be a time when I would want to acquire worldly trappings but it was not just yet.

I went to see Hannah and Igor in their office. It was called Bank Chambers but the branch of the bank had long been closed and replaced by a noodle bar downstairs. It was a typical High Street practice that you can find all over suburban London. All the office furniture was at least slightly shabby and the gold lettering announcing the firm's name on every window was beginning to fade and peel from the sunlight. What had happened to Hannah's ambition? We used to make such grandiose plans together long into the night. We were looking less and less like identical twins. Hannah had her hair now in a naturally curly style cut quite short, which obviously required little work on a daily basis. She had gone in for the Laura Ashley style of voluminous dresses, although hers looked a lot cheaper than the originals. They helped conceal the fact that she was not looking after herself and was putting on weight. I by contrast was dressed as a sharp-suited city slicker in my pinstripe trouser suit. For the moment, I had adopted a very expensive elfin hairstyle which required little daily combing. Come to think of it, I was doing my best to seem as much as possible like a man.

Hannah

Christ! What a contrast! Sophie invited me up to have a look at her office. All glossy palm trees, vast open spaces and white marble slabs. I didn't like the look of the fish, which seemed similar to piranhas, swimming lazily in their huge glass tank: far too much like the clients! Sophie's work station was number thirty-six on the left as you went in. Everything was completely antiseptic and anonymous, without the slightest hint of personal possessions on display. I could not stop thinking of battery hens on a farm. Her little room in the Barbican was no better. I hated that brutalist,

25

cement-based architecture of the 1960s. It was just like the Mappin Terraces in London Zoo. It would have been nice to talk to Sophie to find out how we had moved so far away from each other but she was far too busy and showed no inclination to make time to chat. Somewhat sadly, I descended into the depths of Bank Station to make the journey back to Acton Town, remembering to change to the Piccadilly line at Holborn. Ours were two worlds apart.

Our little takeover was working nicely. The firm gave Igor an expense allowance and he spent his time in the clubs and pubs where the Russians were to be found. Not the big boys: they were out of his league, at least for the time being. Anyway, we could not have handled their work and a small law practice in darkest Ealing would not have satisfied their pretensions. Still, a steady flow of conveyancing, litigation and wills for the Russian community was beginning to stretch the capacity of our little firm to the utmost.

My job was to learn as much as possible during my two-year training contract so as to be able to take over effective running of the firm as soon as I qualified. This was truly learning by doing. I had largely let my brain atrophy at Cambridge as the work required to get my degree was not too demanding, and now I was buzzing on full throttle. So many problems were solvable by common sense or commercial acumen rather than legal knowledge. Fortunately, I seemed to have large supplies of those commodities, certainly not inherited from our parents. Supervision from the partners was totally absent. Old Mr Wills kept his office door firmly shut and seemed to spend most of the working day sleeping. Young Mr Wills arrived at about noon and was usually gone by 3.30 pm. The time in between was spent in his perusal of gardening magazines. I soon learned not to bother him with my petty problems. How he ever absorbed enough law to pass the professional exams was a question that I was incapable of answering, as probably also was he.

The two years passed very quickly. I then theoretically had six months away from the office for the study course leading to the professional exams to qualify as a solicitor. In fact, I was in the office every evening and most weekends to do the work to keep the clients happy. Igor was no help and relations between us were growing more and more strained. His drinks bill to snare an ever-decreasing catch of clients was increasingly inflated and our sex life had dwindled away, not that I had the energy for it. I was saved from an incipient nervous breakdown by the arrival of the exams and I did well enough to pass comfortably. All that practical experience that I had crammed in was a great help.

Mr Wills senior celebrated my qualification as a solicitor by conveniently retiring. I called in the decorators and had his room done up to my taste. Mr Wills junior gave me faint congratulations and also offered to retire. This was not in our grand scheme of things, as we needed a senior lawyer to be the nominal head of the firm according to the Law Society rules. I became his partner on the notepaper but we saw less and less of him in the office. Of course what we were creating was a sham and we would have had difficulty passing a Law Society inspection but there never was one. The rules were designed for the protection of the public to prevent an inexperienced lawyer like me practising alone and getting it wrong. I was confident enough in my own ability to believe that I would not have any problems. Relations with Igor started improving as soon as the exams were over and I regained the energy for sex. We had a wild night of drunken and unprotected sex to celebrate my passing the exams and after it I found that I was pregnant. We decided to get married.

Igor

I was beginning to dislike what I was doing. Being nice to people with whom I had nothing in common, except the drinks I bought them, was not my ideal existence. It was made tolerable by the fact that I was helping Hannah build up her practice. I could lose myself in the passion of our lovemaking sufficiently to forget the banal existence of everyday life. I was also drinking too much to ease the boredom of it all. It suddenly got far worse when Hannah went off to law school to prepare for her professional exams. She was also working in the office every night and every weekend. As a result, she had no time or energy for me. I could no longer get rid of my personal frustrations in her body and I became more and more depressed with the life that I had chosen. I did not know where it was taking me. Fortunately, the exams eventually came to an end and Hannah was interested in me again. I was coming back to life. We had always been very careful about birth control. There was no place for children in our carefully plotted lives together. Then it all changed. We forgot to take precautions on the night that Hannah learned that she had passed her exams and qualified as a solicitor. When she told me she was pregnant, I was overwhelmed with love for her but also fear as to what sort of father I would turn out to be. I need not have worried in that respect.

5

Runnin' Wild

Sophie

It was great to be in London at last. I felt that I had come home, although I did not yet know the city. I set out to remedy that deficiency, guidebook in hand. I found the hardest thing was to link together the various villages that made up the place. It was much simpler underground, but that was taking far too easy an option. My most prized possession was a very expensive pair of trainers in which I could walk comfortably for miles.

I now had the additional letters *LL.M* after my name. My dissertation and the oral examination that followed left me with this further degree but on this occasion with no great academic distinction. I had neither the time nor the energy to do particularly well. It didn't seem to worry anyone except poor Augusta. There were the solicitors' final exams to pass. Being on their fastest track, I was already on the firm's payroll, so I chose the most costly and effective crammers for an intensive six-month course. After that, I came top of the year with first-class honours and won all sorts of prizes. This pleased the firm no end as there was intense rivalry between the big City firms, about to the exam results of their trainees. There was even more intense rivalry within the firm itself. You could cut the political atmosphere with a knife. Everyone in my group was playing politics as a deadly game. The dropout rate was fearsome and having one or more champions in high places helped greatly. I decided to be above or beneath politics, depending on your standpoint. I would do the best possible job I could and always be available for work during the two years of my training contract. If that was not enough to see me through, then so be it. I needed no friends and I made no enemies. There was a lot of social life within the firm: everything from madrigals to Pilates. I smiled sweetly but refused all invitations to join in.

The news that Hannah was pregnant and going to marry Igor caught me in my weak spot. Having been emotionally joined at the hip for such a large part of our lives, we had deliberately divorced when we entered Cambridge. I had been too busy to feel the void but now a huge sense of loss came over me. I missed living side by side with her and sharing every moment as we had done in the old days before we went up to Cambridge. I now needed Hannah and it was a delight and a relief to find she needed me just as much. Our recent differences were forgotten and forgiven. I bought an ancient little red Fiat 500 which had been lovingly restored by its previous owner. It was more a piece of agricultural machinery than an automobile. I kept it in the car park under my block in the Barbican and used it to drive over often to see Hannah in Acton. I felt quite sorry for Igor. Having provided his sperm, there was now no use for him and he kept out of my way when I visited to help Hannah plan the birth and also, of course, the wedding.

Hannah

It was a quiet wedding in the local registry office. Sophie was my maid of honour and Igor actually bought a suit for the occasion. I did nothing to conceal my bump and our aged parents, dragged out of their country retirement, looked suitably bemused. Celebrations in the pub round the corner were hardly consistent with the lavish, lacy white wedding that Sophie and I had planned in the dark nights so many years ago. Igor and I scraped together the money for the deposit on a house in Richmond. The Building Society was falling over itself to lend far more than it should to this newly qualified solicitor and her Russian husband.

There was no time for a honeymoon. We needed to work and develop the practice. In fact, news of my relative competence and efficiency was getting around. What with Igor's Russian introductions, we had more work than we could handle. I bought out the lease of the noodle bar and converted it back to offices. We hired extra staff to fill them to process the work. I was planning to take the minimum time off work to have the baby. We needed the best possible nanny. Sophie was getting increasingly broody as though she was going to have the baby herself and for one mad moment I thought of suggesting that she give up her career and take on the job. We could spend so much more time together. I did not give in to that impulse, which was probably just as well. She almost certainly would have treated the idea with total scorn. If I wanted to settle down to motherhood and married bliss in suburbia, that was my decision. She by contrast was dedicated totally to the life of the single city high flyer, even if she enjoyed taking a little time off to play the role of the loving and totally supportive elder twin sister and aunt-to-be.

Sophie

With Hannah pregnant, the twin thing kicked back into gear with a vengeance. I had heard about husbands suffering sympathetic pregnancy but I was mirroring many of Hannah's symptoms. I had to put on something of an act at work to conceal the fact that I was vastly distracted. During the period of my training contract, my progress through the firm had been spectacular. Like most law firms, mine was divided into various departments to reflect the different types of work undertaken. Training was balanced so that we got experience by time spent in a number of departments for our benefit prior to qualification but not in so many that we were unable to be useful to the firm, particularly once we had grasped the essentials of what was going on. In our firm this gave us three placements of eight months each. Being on the fast track, I was able to choose my placements.

I had started in litigation, where the average entrants can get bogged down in what I call executive photocopying. Litigation is often very labour-intensive, particularly at the lower levels of responsibility and especially when preparing for trial. It is often the fate of the more passive trainees to be burdened with clerical tasks of a very menial and repetitive nature. Computers threaten to make these activities ultimately redundant but they have not yet achieved that result so far. This was not for me and I found myself giving practical and valuable input into some of the firm's most important cases.

I then switched to a corporate group and was immediately engulfed in a multinational takeover of great complexity. It was said that only three people in the firm grasped every ramification and I was one of them. I overstayed in the group for two months as they would not let me go until the job was completed.

I always saw my future in the special projects department and I therefore saved this placement to the last. Lawyers in this group were characterised by their versatility and dedication. You never knew what would be required of you and where you would be needed to perform. A private life with no commitments was almost a prerequisite. I wanted to spend my professional career as a partner involved in this type of work. My renewed close links with Hannah had come at just the wrong time. On qualifying, I had been accepted as a permanent member of the group. Currently we were in a lull and I had time on my hands. It was just as well. This was typical of the work pattern within the department. We were either crazily busy or drawing breath between assignments. By a big stroke of luck, the lull actually lasted until Hannah gave birth.

Bill Ramsden

I had earmarked Sophie Hoare for the department from the time that she came to us at the end of her second year at Cambridge for a summer placement. The only thing that worried me was that she was so damned good-looking that she might get snapped up and deflected into marriage. I required total and ruthless dedication from the people working for me. I need not have worried. Apart from being absolutely brilliant, she showed that complete dedication from the outset. She was always ready for work and seemed to master the most complex case with no effort whatsoever. I could only wish that I had more like her.

Hannah

Charlotte was born effortlessly with Sophie holding my hand and Igor relegated to the hospital waiting room. In spite of everything that was going on around me, I scented trouble but I had reckoned without Sophie's instinctive tact. Having seen me through the birth, she had done her job as my twin sister and just faded away, leaving Igor to again take his place as active husband and father. The overpriced nanny was duly installed and I was back at work within two weeks. Despite what it says in the books in favour of it, breastfeeding was out so far as I was concerned.

Igor

Hannah's pregnancy was a difficult time for me. I felt full of love for her and gratitude, as well as sympathy for the suffering she was experiencing in bearing my child. However, I had to take a back seat as Hannah made it quite clear that she needed and preferred Sophie's company to mine. I had to be very mature and talk to myself very firmly to accept the situation. They say that when you marry one of identical twin girls, you take on two wives. During Hannah's pregnancy, Sophie seemed almost to have taken up residence in our home. She did not so much ignore me as treat me as if I was not there at all. I did my best to merge into the background. Fortunately, soon after Charlotte was born, Sophie's role seemed to end and she was around much less. This meant that I could come out of hiding and resume my role as a loving husband and new father.

Sophie

It was a very strange thing. As soon as Charlotte appeared in the world, I felt a great sense of relief and release, as though I had given birth myself. I had fulfilled my role for Hannah and was now free to resume my own separate existence. I didn't think that Bill Ramsden had noticed my recent drop in dedication and performance. At least, he said nothing and gave no signs that he was concerned. From now on I would be one hundred per cent involved in the job. I threw myself back into work.

6

Love for Sale

Sophie

There was a dark side of my life which was worrying me. When I was at Cambridge, I sometimes felt so sexy in my solitary life that I needed a man. I used to dress down appropriately and go off on my own to one or other of the low pubs in the town, where I always picked someone up quite easily. We would go back to his place if he had one or occasionally to a cheap hotel. On one occasion, we even had sex in the back seat of his car. Thus I relieved myself of my sexual frustrations and I had not had any problems so far. I continued this way of life during the period of my training contract with a few refinements thrown in but now that I was qualified my workload increased considerably and there was no opportunity to make regular visits to Cambridge.

Things were very different now. I had a large salary, money in the bank and a nice home. I had bought the flat in the Barbican where I previously lodged from my landlord who had gone to live abroad permanently. I increasingly needed sex but I wanted no commitment and lacked the time and opportunity to find it.

The problem resolved itself by chance from watching late-night television. I had been in the office far too late one evening and, after heating up a pre-cooked meal in the microwave, I was not yet ready for bed. I switched on randomly to a discussion on male escorts and gigolos for busy professional women. A couple of websites were mentioned and it took me very little research on the internet to track them down. I was worried about laying myself open to blackmail and all sorts of other unpleasant possibilities, so I made unscheduled visits to the addresses shown on both sites. I was reassured by one but less so by the other. The first was rather luxurious, like an upmarket beauty salon. I was encouraged to sign up and state my preferences. Total discretion was assured. All transactions were cash only. The other office was shabby and chaotic but I filed the details away for possible future use.

My first encounter was carefully planned for a Sunday evening after spending the day in Richmond with Hannah and Charlotte. Igor, as usual, kept out of my way. I had booked a double room with king-size bed in one of those large anonymous hotels on the edge of the City which are used by middle-ranking business executives on visits to London. It was important that our encounter took place on neutral ground. The Agency had furnished me with full descriptions and photos of a number of men and I had made my choice. He looked as attractive as any other out-of-work actor hoping to play male leads. I had given the name and address of the hotel together with an approximate meeting time. I had his mobile number, which I was to phone with the room number and exact time.

I arrived early and ran myself a hot bath using my own bath essence rather than the sticky stuff provided by the hotel. I changed into suitably sexy underwear which I had bought specially for the purpose and prepared the room with low lights and perfumed candles, ignoring the smoke alarm above, which fortunately remained silent. I switched on the television and made my way through the film list to the porn section. I chose the most promising title, opened a bottle of champagne from the minibar and lay down on the bed to wait. I suddenly realised that with all my preparations, I had forgotten to phone. I now did so and was not put off by the voice that answered. I was gently playing with myself and in a satisfactory state of arousal when there was a firm knock on the door.

On a cursory glance, he fitted the job description but he seemed as nervous as I inwardly felt. It was up to me to put him at his ease. I suggested that he undress in the bathroom and resumed my pleasurable activities. The film was hardly Oscar material but there was some interesting mass action taking place. I suddenly realised that the bathroom door had opened and he stood there with his well-toned body and scantily attired in a leather posing pouch. He was called Chris and I was called Eve. I had left the considerable sum of money involved in a dish on a bedside table. He slowly counted it and went back to the bathroom to put it in his pocket.

I invited him to join me on the bed and poured him a glass of champagne. We watched the film in silence for some time until I realised that it was up to me to take the initiative if I was going to get my money's worth. I turned to him and started stroking his muscular body. He did the same to me. The contents of his posing pouch were in excellent working order. I pondered fleetingly on how he could perform so readily to order with a complete stranger but I imagined that Viagra and other similar drugs were a great help in his trade. He had used a very pleasant mouthwash and things were progressing nicely as my underwear joined his posing pouch on the carpet. What I liked most of all was being in control. In all my other sexual encounters to date, even if I was in fact the aggressor, I had to preserve the fiction that the big man was taking the lead. 'You Tarzan, me Jane' was invariably the way things worked out. Now I dictated the terms and tempo of the action and my satisfaction was paramount. If I wanted to, I could make him go down on all fours and bark like a dog. The thought made me even hotter. I must say that he responded beautifully to my promptings and I ended in a thoroughly contented and sweaty heap.

I had brought some smoked salmon sandwiches for the afterglow, which we both consumed hungrily. The film reached its climax much later than the two of us and I started thinking that a second round would be most enjoyable. It was still quite early and I would be able to get a good night's sleep before work the next day. It was also within the terms of the contract, my inner lawyer told me, as we had more than an hour to go. The test was whether he had the stamina. It was up to me as the skilful conductor to get the best out of my one-man orchestra. Suffice it to say that I succeeded very well and it all ended in a magnificent crescendo. I would have taken a bow but the only other person in the room was in no fit state to appreciate it.

I allowed him to use the bathroom first and he left with a firm handshake and a most generous tip. He deserved it. I had a short sleep before an invigorating shower. I needed it to get myself into a condition to leave for home. My natural inclination would have been to curl up into a little ball with a contented smile on my face and fall fast asleep for a very long time, exactly where I was lying.

Chris

I was a bit nervous the first few times that I went on dates, as we called them, for the Agency. The particulars and photos that I had to give them were much the same as those required by my theatrical agent. I seemed to have much more success as an escort than as an actor. Roles in that profession for me were few and far between. I had some problems with my partner before I could sign up. He was very jealous at the idea, but I convinced him that having sex with women was merely going through the motions for money and we very much needed more money to support our rather expensive lifestyle and to pay the rent of our overpriced Islington flat. Just as I used the name Adam as an actor, I used Chris for my escort work. My real name is Harvey. When I started after I had passed the medical, I was a bit worried as the gay scene tends to be so promiscuous and I did not want to get into trouble for passing on HIV or AIDS. I was monogamous with Howard and I was pretty sure that he was with me, although he had a lot more time on his hands as he had been out of work for a very long time. We were told by the Agency always to use condoms but you can't be too careful.

I do remember Eve. She was my fourth or fifth date. She had set up the scene nicely and put me at my ease. I had taken Viagra and another blue pill in the car just before, as well as snorting a couple of lines of coke. She was a good-looking woman and I wondered why she needed an escort as she looked as if she could get any man she wanted. She was quite demanding and put me through my paces. I was very tired by the time I left her, clutching a large tip in my hand. At least she was generous. Luckily Howard wanted a quiet night as I don't think I would have been much good for him. All in all, that was one of the better dates. You should see some of them!

Sophie

During the week, I found myself far too often replaying the action in my mind. Various colleagues at work remarked how well I looked. I could hardly wait to do it again and I did the following Sunday. It was not quite as good as the first time. This one lacked stamina and I really had to spur him on to get full value for my money but I was learning some new tricks. It was not the expense, which I could well afford, which troubled me but I felt I was getting hooked on commercial sex which by its very nature was unhealthy. The fact that I could order men in from the Agency on my various business trips abroad just made it worse or better, depending on your point of view. On a job in Berlin, I even experimented with two men at the same time. It was wonderful! I had to admit that where sex was concerned, I enjoyed it most when I was paying for it and in complete control.

7

Makin' Whoopee

Hannah

I had to be careful to massage Igor's fragile ego. He found the 'twin thing' very difficult to handle. Now that Sophie was back regularly in my life, admittedly only on most Sundays and our regular telephone conversations, he seemed to be diminished. I tried to reason with him but he always retreated behind his impenetrable Slavic barrier.

Up to now, he had shown no inclination to visit his homeland but Charlotte was now of an age where travel was relatively easy. I thought that a visit to his family organised by me might help to strengthen our marriage. Igor was so proud of Charlotte that he would enjoy the opportunity to show her off to his relatives.

We flew to St Petersburg and were met by his brother at the airport. The family lived on the outskirts of the city and were by no means rich. We were made welcome but I found the language barrier a problem. It was also very cold. Igor went off hunting with some of his male cousins. I was able to leave Charlotte playing happily with her grandmother and various aunts while exploring, guidebook in hand, the wonders of the Hermitage and the many extraordinary palaces. It was clear that the Russians had an inferiority complex where the French were concerned. They had the money but not the taste. They employed foreign architects and designers to outdo the French. The results were often extravagantly extraordinary and sometimes quite garish. The word 'bling' was not then in use but it described accurately what I was seeing some of the time.

Igor

I sometimes felt, as I mentioned before, that I was married to two women at the same time. I knew that twins were specially linked but until I met Hannah I had no idea of how close the relationship could be. There was definitely a telepathic connection between them, which created a barrier between Hannah and me. To her credit, she was aware of it and at first tried to include me with Sophie but I could not handle it. Perhaps I was too immature. Probably Sophie was a bit jealous of my relationship with Hannah but it seemed to me that she did nothing to make it easy and was always ready to exclude me in conversations by acting as if I wasn't there. It was better for me not to be there, so when Sophie came over I did my best to keep out of their way.

I appreciated Hannah's gesture in organising our trip to St Petersburg. I knew she did it for me but it did not help our relationship. It just made me feel more isolated than ever. I found that I no longer had anything in common with my family. The Russians seemed coarse and uncouth, tending to drink vast quantities of vodka to render themselves insensible as a solution for every problem. The hunting trip was particularly difficult as I knew that it had been organised especially in my honour. To be stuck overnight in a freezing tent, followed by waiting patiently for hours in the cold for some half-starved, mangy animal to come into my sights and be shot, was no longer my idea of pleasure. I was particularly worried that Charlotte was being very spoiled by my mother and sisters, so it was a great relief to bid them all farewell and return home. I could not see us returning.

I didn't much like going out trying to 'pull' Russian clients for Hannah's firm. It had been all right at first but the novelty value had long since worn off. I wished that I hadn't given up my thesis, and I thought about going back into the academic world. At the moment, I much preferred staying at home reading or playing with Charlotte. Claudia, the housekeeper, was so much easier to talk to than Hannah. My wife was so high-powered and she had lost her softness. I put it down to the demands of her job. I think I was a little scared of her. She did not make me feel very masculine, except when we were in bed making love.

Hannah

I could ill afford the week away from the office and returned to relative chaos. Igor's participation and attendance there were becoming increasingly sporadic. He seemed to prefer to spend time at home, which was very much to Charlotte's benefit as he played a lot with her. I was the archetypal working mum rushing out in the morning and struggling to get back for bath time and to read her a story. Very often, after a quick supper I would return to the office for a couple of hours' work uninterrupted by the telephone and other distractions. I really wasn't seeing much of Igor.

I was largely the victim of my own success. New work was coming in based on a job well done and the recommendation of satisfied clients. It may sound arrogant but I was far too good a lawyer to be practising in the suburbs. The immigrant communities, particularly the Indians, quickly discovered that I could give them the service that they needed speedily and at reasonable prices calculated on the time I spent. My very success based on my previous efficiency if things continued as they were, because of an excess of work, would inevitably lead to inefficiency. I put the problem to Igor but he was no help. He was uncoupled from reality and sought refuge from the problems of life in his books and by caring for Charlotte.

Up to now, I had handled everything that came through the door with the help of such staff as I could recruit. One problem was that most good lawyers aspired to work in the City or Central London, if only for the reason that the lunchtime shopping was so much better. I had to design attractive packages for women lawyers who were mothers, lived in the area and wanted to work fewer hours only, so that they could spend more time with their children. That way I could recruit quality lawyers. The same applied to other staff. Once again, word of mouth soon meant that I was able to up the standard of those I employed. A lot of my part-time workers were relatively far more productive than the full-timers whom they replaced.

I also had to take a long, hard look at the work that we did. I got my accountant to do a profitability analysis. I realised that I had to take pruning shears to a lot of the types of law that we practised. Historically, we had always had some clients on legal aid. They had to go. The behaviour of some of the legal aid clients was deplorable. Because it was a free service, a number of them saw no need to keep appointments or otherwise treat me with respect. I sympathised with my medical friends in the National Health Service. The final straw was when the daughter of a legal aid client complained to the Law Society because we had misspelled her father's name in a letter! She should have been happy that we were dealing with his case at all. It was not economic for us because the Legal Aid Fund paid miserably low hourly rates, far less than the fee-paying clients. We had done enough charitable work. If I wanted to take on a case for free because it interested me or I felt that it was a particularly worthy cause, that was an entirely different matter and my choice alone. We had never gone in for 'no win, no fee' work. Frankly, I found the whole idea of it unsavoury and only likely to drag down the ethical and moral standards of the legal profession. Instead of viewing the client's case dispassionately and professionally, you became commercially interested and a partner in the financial outcome of the case, thus losing all professional objectivity. I felt that I had little in common with those in that type of practice. So many were little more than ambulance-chasers.

Next to go was all crime and general litigation. There was too much time wasted hanging around in court, waiting for the cases to be called. My lawyers' time could be used far more productively sitting in the office in front of their computer screens. I was making a name for myself as the divorce queen of West London and that, henceforth, was to be my sole area of practice. There were plenty of reasonably wealthy clients who did not want to travel all the way into Central London and pay the exorbitant fees of the specialist lawyers there. I could even offer valet parking, having done a special deal with a nearby parking lot. I suspected that the owners were Albanian mafia but that did not concern me unduly. They certainly did a wonderful job of polishing my car daily. Practising family law coupled with running the firm was enough to keep me frantically busy.

I had plenty of good lawyers to do the property work, both residential and commercial. Frankly, that work bored me but it was still lucrative despite competitive pressures. The clients were prepared to pay for personal service and extra effort rather than be lost in the battery-hen-style conveyancing factories that had sprung up. Probate, wills and trusts completed the menu that we offered. There was always good money to be made out of the dead. I had a bit of a mental struggle with myself over corporate and commercial work. It could be very lucrative, even in Ealing but I felt that the resources that I would have to deploy to do it properly would take up too much personnel and precious space. I also felt that the intensity of the work made it unsuitable for part-time lawyers. I therefore reluctantly decided to farm it out on a case-by-case basis to various appropriate law firms both locally and more centrally on the tacit understanding that they would reciprocate by shovelling the work my way that they were conflicted from undertaking themselves.

While all this was going on, Mr Wills junior was continuing to come to the office daily for a few meagre hours without any perception of how the firm was changing around him. I did sit down with him and discuss his financial needs and resources for the future. It would only be a few more years before his allotment claimed him full-time. I coveted his office for more productive staff but I would have to wait.

Frankly, as a source of introductions Igor was of little use to me any longer but it did not matter as we had all the business we could handle. I had to work to see that we maintained an active marriage. It was a bit mechanical but I arranged that Saturday night was our sex night. We would go to the local Indian restaurant and consume a bottle of red wine with our curry. I would transform our bedroom into a temple of Asian delights as the mood took me and I have to say that Igor was still a very satisfactory lover even if he did require a certain amount of coaxing from me to get him to the point.

I'm not sure if I really wanted another child – life was already complicated enough – but I became rather lax on the precautions front and found myself pregnant again. Sophie once more became a wonderful aunt-to-be and a terrific active twin sister. It was as though my pregnancy switched her on like an electric light. In many ways we were closer than we had ever been. I knew that she had an immensely demanding job but I grieved that it left her no time for a normal social life of her own. There should have been a good man in her life. I wished I could introduce her to one but I knew none remotely suitable and felt that she would summarily reject them anyway.

I had plenty of time to make preparations for the birth and I even hired a locum for the office so that this time I could take a full three months off if I was so inclined. I was lucky once again to have an easy pregnancy. I worked right up to the last possible moment and briefed the staff with copious notes so that my absence would be felt as little as possible. Darling Sophie came rushing in at the last moment from some assignment abroad to hold my hand and mop my brow as I went into labour. Ivan was born exactly two years after Charlotte. It made it much simpler only to have to remember one birthday and they could share parties. As soon as Sophie appeared, Igor went skulking off, heaven knows where. I only wished that the two adults closest to me could find a way of getting on better together but I had much more pressing and important things to think about.

Igor

Our marriage was becoming increasingly difficult. What I had liked so much about Hannah was her enthusiasm for life and the law, coupled with a burning desire to help people in need. This was now replaced by a much colder and more calculating attitude to what she did professionally. I suppose I had not really grown up and was still a bit of a naive student at heart. I so much enjoyed Charlotte's childish innocence and I spent endless hours in her company. I felt that Hannah had lost hers. I still loved her very much but I felt in awe of her and inferior to her. She was so masculine in her attitude and outlook.

Saturday nights were my chance to show my love for her and give her sexual satisfaction. The problem was that I was increasingly feeling that that was my sole role in the marriage. She no longer needed the clients that I brought in, so I reduced my efforts to charm the Russian community. Frankly this was a relief as I was feeling more and more like a prostitute. I was reading a lot of history and philosophy but I had not yet found the inspiration to restart my academic career. As I have already mentioned, the idea of a visit to my family in Russia was all Hannah's. I knew it was meant to give me pleasure but all I felt was alienation from the Russian way of life. I realised how far apart I had grown from my family and I knew the visit would not be repeated and they were never likely to seek us out. I had no roots any more.

At the same time, I realised that I was lapsing into a Russian-style version of self-pity. I had chosen life in the West. I had to adopt some of its optimism rather than the pessimism of my mother country. I had to appreciate how lucky I was, make the best of my life and enjoy my family. I needed to adopt some of Hannah's positive outlook on life. I resolved to make an appointment to visit Cambridge to see my former director of studies with a view to reviving my unfinished thesis. With my subsequent experiences of life, I could perhaps give it a new and more interesting slant.

8

Changing Partners

Sophie

I had chosen to do the most demanding work in the most demanding department of the top firm in London. We were not the biggest, but we were acknowledged by those in the know as the best. It was just as well that I had such a restricted social life as the calls on my time never seemed to end. I would finish one all-consuming project only to find another file marked *MOST URGENT* waiting on my desk. The gaps between assignments were getting ever shorter. I tried to keep most Sundays clear to visit Richmond to see Hannah and Charlotte and then later for my clandestine hotel action. This latter had exposed how physically unfit I was. To enjoy it more, I needed to tone up considerably, so I joined a local gym which opened at six in the morning. You would find me there at opening time every day except Monday. I needed a couple of hours' extra rest after the hectic activities of the night before.

There was no chance of being bored with the work. I could be investigating a bank fraud in Singapore one week in conjunction with local lawyers and accountants. The next, I could be in a small town in the north of England looking at irregular patterns of voting fraud under conditions of the utmost secrecy. I kept several bags ready packed with different weights of clothing for varying climates. I had to be ready to travel at very short notice. While the work was normally based on English law, I often had to consider the impact of foreign laws. I was no linguist but the type of work I was undertaking meant that money was of no object so I had the best translators available. There was often an element of secrecy and even danger in what I did. I was used to being whisked off in a jeep surrounded by heavily armed bodyguards in the pitch-dark and freezing desert to reach some godforsaken oil well to meet some heavily disguised foreign potentate. That said, there were plenty of weeks when I was chained to my desk, going laboriously through documents either on the screen or in paper form, trying to cross-reference and find obscure linkages. The continual battle to keep up with and make use of advances in modern technology was one which I found particularly exhausting. The firm employed the brightest and best in its IT department and I was constantly liaising with them. At the same time, I was mindful of making sure that I did not get so bogged down in the mysteries of IT that I missed the point of what I was doing. I felt that a number of my colleagues and opponents were guilty of that sin.

I was clearly advancing up the ladder of seniority within the firm. When I started, there was plenty of supervision but now I was trusted to do the work on my own. If I wanted advice and I was not so stupid as to fail to seek it if I needed it, Bill Ramsden and the other partners were always very helpful and supportive. The firm's resources were readily available to me and now I could pick my own teams on an ad hoc basis to help me in the work if they were needed. My reputation in the business was becoming well established and I received several discreet approaches from headhunters on behalf of other practices but I was not interested. I was already at the best firm doing the highest quality work for the most important clients and I was being very well paid for doing it.

Jeremy King, King Executive Search

Sophie Hoare was high on my list. She had been asked for by several rival firms and I had tried to make the initial connection but without any success. The way to do it is to get hold of their mobile phone number. You then call them when they are out of the office. This can be difficult with some as they seem to spend all their time there. You tell them that a prestigious outfit has expressed an interest in meeting them with a view to offering them a position leading speedily to partnership. Most will be sufficiently interested to take the bait and go for the initial interview, if only to use the outside interest to secure a better deal with their existing employers. The secret is to find the right moment to make the approach, when they are doing well but feel unappreciated and the road leading to partnership seems endless or blocked completely. I must be pretty good at finding that moment as I drive a new Maserati. However, in Sophie's case I got nowhere. She was always polite but not interested.

Sophie

There was only one possible reason why I would want to move: more speedy partnership prospects. The partnership track at my firm was a minimum of seven years. I was fiercely ambitious and wanted to abridge that to five years in my case. I would be a pioneer in that respect. I was not exaggerating in thinking that some of the work I was doing for the partnership was unique. I had invented or developed new techniques for doing it which were reflected in the enormous fees that I was bringing in. There was only one area where I was not contributing and that was the introduction of new clients. At this stage, I did not see that there was much I could do about it. My rates were such that the only clients who could afford my services were governments, large corporations, mega-wealthy individuals and the most powerful non-governmental organisations. My job, as I saw it, was to delight or at least to maintain a satisfied client who would come back to us for more.

Bill Ramsden

I watched with fascination the whirlwind progress through the firm of Sophie Hoare. There was plenty of brain power within the organisation but nobody else seemed to harness it so effectively. She was very much the subject of speculation at partners' lunches. With a considerable number of women partners now in the firm, this could no longer get out of hand as in the old, male-dominated days but partners of both sexes were equally puzzled. All agreed that she was very beautiful and always perfectly turned out. She seemed to dedicate herself totally to the work of the department and its clients with no obvious time or opportunity for extracurricular activities. No one could fault her conduct within the firm: she was uniformly pleasant, if somewhat distant and impersonal in her dealings with everyone, to the point that she had neither friends nor enemies. In other words, she was too good to be true.

It fell to me as her supervising partner to exercise a little pastoral care and invite her out to lunch. In these days where anything can be construed as sexual harassment, it was not wise to be unaccompanied, so I asked Elizabeth Jones to come along as well. Although in a different department, Elizabeth was a recently promoted partner whose qualities in many respects mirrored those of Sophie. In an ideal world, I would have had a constant dialogue with Sophie as to her ambitions and intentions but we were all so busy to get the work done that this was impossible.

My PA selected a quiet table in a restaurant overlooking the river and the three of us sat down as virtual strangers, though we had worked together cheek by jowl for a number of years. We asked Sophie what she wanted, although it was by no means put so bluntly. The answer came back loud and clear: a partnership in the firm. Sophie had nearly completed five years as a qualified lawyer with us. I told her that she would have to wait a minimum of two more years. The answer came back that she wanted it now. I had difficulty avoiding catching Elizabeth's eye but we both knew what message we had to carry back to the partnership. We would have to weigh up the risk of losing her to the competition who did not have such rigorous standards for partnership, against breaking existing rules and establishing a precedent. There was no doubt in either of our minds that she was well worth it.

We then had a general discussion about her need to integrate, rather than ingratiate, herself more into the firm prior to becoming a partner. Her only concession was to agree to join the Pilates group. Frankly, the need for collegiality had slipped in recent years as the demand of ever more effective work production had increased. There had been a time when the partners' dining room had resembled the senior common room of an Oxbridge college but that was some time ago. There were now quite a few oddballs and social misfits among the partners. The modern criterion was performance above everything else.

Elizabeth Jones

I wonder what an inquisitive third party would have thought of our little lunch group. In the middle was Bill, immensely tall with greying hair and matinee idol good looks. He was flanked by two beautifully groomed and attractive women. If an attempt was made to place us, the likely conclusion was that we were a red-hot media group who had somehow strayed from the West End to the City. We certainly did not fit the stereotypes of City solicitors.

There was something larger than life about Sophie Hoare. She was just too perfect. It was as if she were playing the role of an aspiring woman partner in a law firm in accordance with some kind of script written for a television play. I sensed that there were inner tensions and conflicts that we were not allowed to see. It would not surprise me at all if she blew up and had some sort of nervous breakdown within the next five years or so. She was driving herself too hard. Nevertheless, I was prepared to support her application for early partnership. I was on a personal crusade to increase the number of women partners in the firm. Parity was my ultimate aim. It was good for our reputation in the City that we were at the forefront of the drive towards gender equality. I knew that Sophie would not be one of those of us trying to change the atmosphere in the partners' dining room from that of a traditional men's club but that was not the most important consideration. That task could be left to others.

Sophie

I may have been a bit too direct at lunch. I knew why Bill and Elizabeth had asked me out. If I had had a female role model in the firm, it would have been Elizabeth. She was very beautiful and always perfectly groomed and with the sharpest possible intellect. They asked me what I wanted. No point beating about the bush. I told them: a partnership. I knew about the seven-year rule but I wanted it in five. I felt I deserved it. They were both far too civilised to show shock. I knew Elizabeth had waited seven years for her partnership. Conversation moved on to how I could integrate better within the firm. Frankly, I felt I gave enough of myself to it already. My only concession was to agree to join the Pilates group, which met two mornings a week. It would make a nice change from sweating away in the gym every morning at the crack of dawn.

I had to wait another four months for the announcement, two

months over my chosen five-year span. There were six new partners on the list. I was one of them! I immediately phoned Hannah. She was over the moon. My next call was to the Agency. Could they provide a man at very short notice? Indeed they could, albeit at double the normal price. I gave myself a night to remember. I deserved it.

9

Groovin' High

Hannah

I lasted at home for two months before the call of the office became too much for me. Ivan was at first a very placid child and I even enjoyed breastfeeding while I stayed home but I stopped completely as soon as I went back to work: no half measures for me. Sophie came round every Sunday when she was not on business abroad. She really played the part of an excellent aunt for both children and lifted my spirits with every visit. If I had ever had doubts, this period at home made me realise that full-time motherhood was not for me. The office had run extremely smoothly in my absence. The very expensive locum had done a good job and I seamlessly settled into my working life again. That is what I truly enjoyed.

I was thrilled by Sophie's news about her partnership. I always knew that my sister was an exceptional lawyer but her rapid promotion meant that she was the best of the bunch. We celebrated with champagne and even Igor kept a smile on his face throughout. Charlotte thought that it was a grown-up birthday party but I found it too difficult to explain what we were celebrating. She knew it wasn't mine or Sophie's birthday as we always had a double celebration. I left her with her illusion, although she could not understand why there were no candles on the cake.

Igor's promised flood of Russian clients had long been merely a trickle. When I saw that he had written a Russian-sounding name in my appointments diary, I was not expecting very much. The surname sounded rather familiar but I gave it no further thought at the time. There was already too much on my mind.

Igor

If I thought that Hannah's second pregnancy would bring out her motherly instincts to the exclusion of her desire to keep working, I was wrong. It was just the same as before: Sophie rode to the rescue and I was banished to the kitchen. They were as thick as thieves. I could see a lot of me in Ivan. He was much less emotionally volatile than Charlotte and rather a solemn child, though physically very active. I was with them both for most of the week but gave them up almost every Sunday so that Hannah and Sophie could have their time with them. It was not that Hannah was a bad mother; far from it. It was just that active motherhood was low on her list of priorities. I was determined to fill the gap as a hands-on father.

I was increasingly neglecting my Russian contacts, so it was something of a surprise to receive a call out of the blue from one of my former drinking partners. Alexei was very much a fixer within the community. He knew everybody and everyone knew him. He had the reputation of sometimes straying on the wrong side of the law but he was a useful man to know. He could get you a new washing machine at wholesale cost or prime seats at a sold-out boxing match (in the latter case, at much-enhanced prices). He asked if we could meet in the greatest secrecy. The wife of one of the top oligarchs, someone way above both our leagues, needed legal representation in a most difficult case. She had chosen my wife as the person to act for her and needed my personal introduction. I said that I could see no problem with this and then, with maximum dramatic effect, he uttered the name Bronia Seratov. Everyone in the Russian community and far beyond knew the name Seratov. It was almost the Russian equivalent of the House of Windsor.

"She wants a divorce," he went on.

Seratov v Seratov would be the biggest heavyweight bout that you could get.

Hannah

Bronia Seratov arrived outside our offices like visiting royalty in a chauffeur-driven Rolls-Royce accompanied by two black Range Rovers, one in front and the other behind, with darkened windows and heaven knows how many bodyguards and security men inside. She swept into the office, ignoring the motley, informal guard of honour that Igor had assembled on the pavement outside, in a swirl of furs and a haze of perfume. She was nearly as tall as me and had obviously been very beautiful but good living was beginning to blur the sharp outline of her glorious figure. I doubted if she was naturally as spectacularly blonde as she appeared and she clearly had had very expensive work done by the best cosmetic surgeons.

Igor's services as an interpreter were not required as she spoke fluent if strongly accented English, so he left us to it. I gently suggested that it was unwise to leave her vehicles on the double yellow line outside our office and that safe parking could be arranged around the corner, though I feared that my Albanians might be tempted to make off with such expensive cars. My views were dismissed with a wave of a well-manicured hand. It seemed that the Seratovs were immune from the traffic regulations that plagued us lesser mortals.

"I want you to act for me on my divorce," she began without any preliminaries. "I got your name from several of my friends and also from my hairdresser."

With recommendations like those, I was left speechless.

"My husband can afford the best." She mentioned certain well-known names. "I don't care. I think you can do a good job for me even if you practise in the sticks. Do you think you can handle it? You know who you are up against."

I felt a little bit like Avis in the advertisement compared with Hertz: the second best desperately trying to keep up with the very best. I just had to try a little harder. Having put me at my ease, which was the opposite of the normal lawyer/client relationship, we got down to business.

Bronia came from an underprivileged background. She was clever at school and worked hard, leading to further education. As a student beauty queen at Moscow University, she had had the pick of the young men. In what was very much a man's world, she had started her own property business just as things became more relaxed politically and economically and she was buying and selling on her own account, as well as acting as an agent for others.

Oleg Seratov also came from an undistinguished family but she was attracted to his drive and ambition as well as his good looks. He was five years older than she and already well established in a small way as a businessman prepared to wheel and deal in whatever commodities were available to him. Some of his close contemporaries were beginning to make names for themselves in the new Russian politics. If they continued to climb, there was no reason why he should not rise with them if he obeyed the rules of the game. It was all about whom you knew rather than what you knew. It was important that they all got rich together.

Bronia and Oleg decided to live together and initially had an impoverished existence in a freezing-cold apartment on the seventeenth floor of one of those faceless blocks with an elevator which rarely worked. After she graduated, they married and Bronia took a job as a receptionist in the head office of one of Moscow's principal banks. Her salary was very welcome as Oleg was finding short-term profitable deals hard to come by at that particular moment in the expansion of Russian capitalism.

Then came perestroika and glasnost. The great sell-off by President Yeltsin of state industries to the private sector was underway and Oleg was perfectly positioned to benefit. He had powerful political patrons and a web of contacts in high places, together with friends that mattered seemingly everywhere. Bronia was a great help. One of the senior managers in her bank took a shine to her and she led him on beautifully without ever compromising herself. It was always a case of 'jam tomorrow'. She introduced Oleg to her aspiring lover and he was only too eager to finance Oleg's enterprises. With unlimited funds and much goodwill in the right quarters, Oleg bought up state industries indiscriminately. He knew what bribes had to be promised and paid to which intermediaries by some kind of sixth sense. There was a quasi-arithmetical formula involved: the larger the bribes, the cheaper the price of the targeted business relative to its true worth. Cash was king and the envelope was soon replaced by the suitcase, which in turn was replaced by whole fleets of lorries filled with the stuff. A number of politicians and state employees became very rich overnight and a number of would-be capitalists found themselves as proprietors of the great businesses of the State, for which they had paid nothing like the true value. As usual, the overall losers were the Russian people.

It all happened so quickly that Oleg and Bronia found it difficult to comprehend what and how much they owned and where it all was. It included transport and haulage businesses and airlines, various mines producing vital minerals, factories of all sorts, hotels, office buildings, and much land for future development. By tacit agreement among these new oligarchs, there were certain areas of business that were off limits. For example, the Seratovs would not involve themselves in the business of energy and steel. Conversely, they did not expect to be challenged in transport or airlines. There was a form of honour among thieves.

The problem was that a new breed of even more predatory gangsters had grown up and a number of the original buyers of state assets were speedily stripped of their purchases. Oleg was determined to see that did not happen to him. Bronia left her job with the bank. Her putative lover had served his purpose and could be left to contemplate how much he had done to receive so little in return. The apartment was abandoned overnight and they moved to a somewhat dilapidated mansion on the outskirts of Moscow, which had the benefit of high walls. It was in the portfolio of properties of one of the businesses which Oleg had almost accidentally acquired. A newly owned construction company was put to work to bring the mansion up to the condition of luxury that befitted one of Russia's foremost new oligarchs. Lastly and of greatest importance, a host of security guards were hired to make sure that what had been so hastily gained could not be brutally snatched away. They also had a great fear of personal kidnap with their new status and wealth.

There was plenty for Bronia to do to help consolidate their new empire. Her economics degree was complemented by her good business brain but in their new environment of abundant wealth and luxury she felt sufficiently relaxed to allow herself to become pregnant. Vassily was followed little more than a year later by Natasha. Bronia was still engaged in the business in that Oleg continued to discuss strategy with her and take her advice but she had given up her day-to-day involvement. The money was rolling in. They travelled everywhere by private jet and they had added a mansion in London and penthouses in New York and Monaco to their list of homes. A suitably large and luxurious yacht was in the course of construction, to be moored within view of their home on the Riviera. The only asset missing was ownership of an English Premier League football club. Oleg had put in several bids but so far he had been thwarted. He felt the lack very keenly as competition between the top oligarchs was bitterly intense: ostentation and appearance were everything.

Bronia's days and nights were busy. She liked to be a hands-on mother, although she had all the home help that she could possibly want. A number of the oligarchs had already exchanged their wives for more up-to-date models as the original ones were not up to standard and had passed their sell-by date. She started with certain built-in advantages but she was not one to rest on her laurels. Her expenditure on clothes and jewellery was fully commensurate with her status, as was the time and money spent on her various beauty treatments. She had to be ready with her bags packed to fly at a moment's notice to any part of the world, with or without the children. Just keeping their various homes running was a full-time job. Who says that the life of an oligarch's wife is all languorous leisure?

I must say that I was beginning to wonder when she was going to get to the point and tell me why she was really here. What she was telling me was all good background stuff but I had never before been subjected to such a continuous barrage of words. She paused suddenly and looked at her incredibly expensive watch. I had seen one like it in a glossy magazine in my dentist's waiting room but I had no idea of the make or the price. I was sure it was the real thing rather than a cheap Hong Kong substitute.

"My God! It is six o'clock and I've been talking non-stop. I must go and get ready for a charity dinner." She fished in her glossy Chanel handbag and brought out a chequebook. "Let me pay you for your time. How much do I owe you?"

It was good news that she was aware of the basis on which I charged, if not yet the hourly rate I was intending to employ. I told her that she could settle up next time she came.

"Can I come again tomorrow at the same time?"

"It's a date," I exhaustedly assured her.

10

Wild Man Blues

Hannah

I had a lot to think about, not least a call from Mrs Wills junior. The doctor had told her that her husband should not go into work any more as it was causing him too much stress. I could not imagine how stress came into the equation as he did no noticeable work while he was in the office. Nevertheless, I received her news with gratitude as I needed the extra office space, especially in view of the human bombshell which had hit me today. On the basis that Bronia Seratov was indeed a long-term client, I had to free myself from a lot of work for others so that I could be available to absorb in future her heavy demands on my time. I was already in touch with two first-rate women divorce lawyers who matched my job criteria. Both were aching to leave full-time domesticity. The only constraint had been lack of space and now that problem was solved. I had already made arrangements with Mr Wills junior to put him on half pay when his time came to retire. It was not much, so all I had to do was inform the bank to reduce his monthly payments. He had been a very useful shadow principal while I needed one but now I was sufficiently long-qualified to stand on my own feet and fulfil the Law Society criteria to be a sole practitioner.

I knew that I was going to have an extra-long telephone conversation that night with Sophie. I needed to tell her all that had happened today and to seek her advice. She was a partner in a big firm and I was the principal of a small firm. I was faced with taking on the type of case which was normally only dealt with by the former. How much should my new hourly rate be for Bronia? Certainly a lot more than the rate at which I charged my average Ealing clients but not quite as much as the City and West End lawyers expected to receive. After all, they had much higher overheads.

Sophie

I was thrilled at Hannah's news. I had been a partner long enough now to have some idea of the inner workings and economics of law practice. While the firm did no divorce or family work, it was easy to get introductions to some of the top divorce solicitors on the old girls' network. Everyone was surprisingly open and forthcoming. I had everything Hannah needed to know by lunchtime the next day. They say that it is only men who are good at networking. That's no longer the case. Perhaps it is because there are still so few of us at the top level that women do so well on that front.

Lady Harriet Fanshawe

Hannah Hoare would never have telephoned me to ask for advice. I was a hotshot divorce lawyer in Central London at the top of the tree. She was an up-and-coming divorce lawyer in Ealing. A cat does not talk to a queen or ask her for information. However, a call from her sister Sophie was something else. She told me that she had been recommended to call me by a mutual friend. She then mentioned that she was a partner in a top City firm. They did no family work. On the basis that one good turn deserves another, if I answered all her questions, I was likely to receive some juicy referrals. Nothing more was said but the message was implicit. I told her everything her sister needed to know. Who says the old girls' network doesn't exist? You scratch my back and I'll scratch yours.

Hannah

The convoy drew up just as it had the previous day and bang on time. Bronia was wearing a new and extremely pungent scent. Out came the chequebook and she informed me that she wanted to pay me a substantial amount on account of costs by way of a retainer to secure my exclusive services. Armed with the information that Sophie had given me, I suggested a figure which was more than the whole firm's fees put together for the last half-year. Without turning a hair, she wrote out the cheque. Tonight she had no other engagements and she could stay until eight o'clock if that was convenient for me. After making one phone call home, I assured her that it was.

Bronia wasted no more time, but plunged back into her story. I was making detailed notes. Oleg was travelling a lot to the various far-flung outposts of his vast business empire. Sometimes she did not see him for weeks on end but they kept in touch with daily or nightly lengthy phone calls. He was still seeking her advice on strategic issues of the business. When they were together, life consisted of a hectic round of charity balls, dinners and parties. The contrasts in her life rather suited her as she was able to give far more care and attention to the children, with the help of the legion of nannies and other staff, when Oleg was away. There was absolutely no sign whatsoever that there was anything wrong with the marriage. Oleg was his usual loving and thoughtful self, always bringing her back expensive and unusual gifts from his trips, and their sex life continued to be explosive when they were together.

The whole family were sitting at breakfast in their London home a few days before our meeting when there was a sudden ring at the front door. Bronia was surprised that Oleg jumped up with alacrity to answer it, as though he was expecting the caller and needed to greet him himself. There were plenty of servants available to do the job and no need for him to involve himself. He returned with a nondescript-looking man in a shabby dark suit who was carrying a sheaf of papers in his right hand. These he gave to Bronia. Oleg immediately ushered him out and resumed his seat at the breakfast table as though nothing had happened. Bronia was thunderstruck to discover that she was holding Oleg's petition for divorce against her, based on her alleged unreasonable behaviour, fictional evidence of which seemed to go on for pages.

If Oleg was not expecting a violent reaction he must have been stupid. Bronia exploded in hysterical tears and screams. Fortunately, a nanny was on hand to take the children away before they heard and saw too much. In one of the exhausted intervals of Bronia's tirade, Oleg announced in a calm voice that he was moving out into an apartment. He managed to leave the room without suffering physical violence, though if he had delayed a bit longer, Bronia assured me, that she was capable of doing him considerable damage.

She quickly realised the loneliness and vulnerability of her position. Here she was living in luxury in London while her family, to whom she was not close anyway, were thousands of miles away in Moscow. Such friends as she had here were social friends only and not the kind in whom she felt happy to confide or, if she did, expressed a clear desire not to be involved as soon as they realised that they would be taking sides against one of the most powerful and aggressive of the oligarchs.

The children had been enrolled in an English private school, and here she found the answer. She sought help from the mothers of her children's school friends. One Russian woman led her to Igor via Alexei and no fewer than three others mentioned my name as the lawyer who could help, as of course did her hairdresser.

The story – with embellishments, some tears, diversions and interruptions – had taken us to eight o'clock. I felt emotionally exhausted, while Bronia seemed positively to thrive on the experience. She looked as fresh as a daisy. We agreed to meet two hours earlier the next day and I was left to read the petition for divorce. If the story that Bronia had told me was true, it would be a masterly work of fiction. Her nightly revelations were beginning to remind me of the storyteller in the *Arabian Nights* leaving his audience aching to hear more after every episode.

11

Let's Call the Whole Thing Off

Sophie

I was very much enjoying our late-night chats and felt I was truly able to help Hannah. I knew little about divorce law but I had the big firm experience that she lacked, while divorce had very much become her speciality. There was not that much difference in the strategy and tactics involved with some of the work that I did. If we needed help, my informal network of women lawyers in the City was available to her.

Hannah

I read carefully the divorce petition that Bronia had handed me. It was a bulky document as the list of items of unreasonable behaviour was extensive but frankly they were all rather flimsy. I viewed the petition rather like the opening gambit in a game of chess. Oleg clearly wanted out of the marriage. My gut feeling was that he had met a woman and wanted to replace Bronia with a more up-to-date model like so many of his fellow oligarchs. He knew her pride would be hurt and he calculated that she would not wish to stay in a marriage where she was not wanted. If other terms could be agreed, I felt that the existing grounds for divorce would by consent be replaced by something much more neutral, perhaps Oleg's admitted adultery. I suspected that agreeing the other terms would be a big, big problem.

I hoped that there would not be a great fight over the children. Bronia was in a very volatile state and if Oleg tried to deny her residence or custody, she was likely to fly off the handle. His lifestyle was such that I could not see how he could demand residence but I had seen too many fathers treat their children as unfeeling possessions in this type of situation and fight for custody even if it was in no way in the best interests of the children. If she was not put under pressure in this area, I reckoned that Bronia's motherly instincts would prevail and she would want the children to continue to be involved with their father and have generous contact or access with him, particularly if he made and maintained lavish financial provision for them, which he could well afford. In other words, he would get what he paid for.

It was on overall financial issues that I could see the big fight looming. I had not even begun to go into these matters with Bronia. She had not been the typical trophy wife of a rich man by any means but had involved herself from the outset as a significant partner in her husband's business. It was only the arrival of the children which had lessened her role, although he still looked to her for advice on strategy, if her version of events was to be believed. She had told me her story without being aware of its significance… or was she cleverer than I thought?

Oleg's behaviour over the service of the divorce petition led me to think that he would be devious and tricky on money matters as well. For so many businessmen when their marriages collapsed, their natural instincts were to treat the wife merely as a failed investment and cut their losses accordingly. This looked to me to be a classic case where the wife should receive half the assets. She had been business partner, lover, wife, homemaker, hostess and mother. The problem was likely to be in identifying the assets and enforcing any court orders. The original fortune had arisen in Russia. Other assets had been acquired elsewhere including in the UK but I had a feeling that I was very much out of my depth. International asset-tracing was not something that was meat and drink to the average Ealing solicitor. I badly needed to talk to Sophie.

Sophie

Wow! My little sister was certainly in at the deep end. One big question was whether Mrs Seratov had access to sufficient money to fund the campaign that was likely to be required to get her rightful share of the assets. I could see that Hannah could do quite a lot of work while leaving her bills unpaid in the expectation that she would be well remunerated when Bronia's money eventually rolled in. But how long would she have to wait? How long is a piece of string? However, if she did too much without being paid, she could wreck her practice and go bankrupt. She still had her own bills to pay.

The problem was that she would have to surround herself with top experts to help her, including barristers, accountants, valuers and asset-tracers of all kinds. They were extremely likely to be unwilling to leave their fees outstanding on a delayed basis and Hannah needed urgently to sit down with her client and talk about what money was available. I knew that contingent fees (no win, no fee) were not allowed in divorce work. Even if they were and I could envisage crafty ways of working on a double-or-quits basis, who in their right mind would take the risk when dealing with a slippery and powerful customer like Oleg Seratov, with his assets concealed all over the place?

12

Give Me Money, That's What I Want

Hannah

The next day's session with Bronia was even more gruelling than those that had gone before. I needed to get a picture of the joint assets and liabilities. She had an excellent business brain and was able to give me a great deal of information but the more I learned, the more I realised what a huge task I had taken on. Oleg had an almost paranoid fear of his assets being discovered. Bronia put this down to concern regarding other oligarchs knowing too much about his business, or the Russian state turning hostile and wishing to expropriate what he had if he were to displease someone at or near the top who had the power to do so, the President for example, as others had done. Easy come, easy go. I suggested that he might have been trying to make it difficult for his wife to recover what was due to her. Everything had its ownership cloaked in a chain of offshore companies. For example, their Kensington mansion was owned by a Panamanian company whose bearer shares were held by a Lichtenstein *Anstalt*, which in turn was owned by a Jersey trust.

Bronia warned me that her knowledge might not be completely up to date as Oleg loved tinkering with things and changing them around. Now that he had moved out, they were no longer in contact and there was an ever-widening rift between them, this was increasingly likely.

I now had to turn to the more delicate subject of how she was going to pay for what looked like it would become a lengthy and complex litigation involving asset-tracing and enforcement in many different countries.

"Please forgive me, but we need to talk about the question of costs: how you are going to pay for all this? At the end of the day, we should end up with an order from the court for your husband to pay a substantial part of your costs but the reality is that those advising you, including barristers, accountants and me, need to be paid as we go along." I tentatively opened the discussion. "We can't just wait until the end."

"Don't worry," answered Bronia. "I was expecting this. I can't let you work for nothing. I know that you have bills to pay too."

I breathed an inward sigh of relief. At least she had a basic grasp of our economics and cash flow needs but did she have the money?

"Before I met Oleg, I ran my own property business in Moscow and I have always insisted on my financial independence," she continued. "I have the equivalent of over a million pounds in a bank in Zurich and I also own two large chalets in Davos, which are let all year round and produce a substantial net income. Both properties are free of mortgage. Will that be enough?"

I tried not to smile. "I would not be surprised if your husband tries to kill you with the cost of the litigation – he will not be the first – but you certainly have enough to be getting on with. You should be able to prevent that from happening."

Bronia was beginning to look impatient, as though she wanted us to get on to more important matters but I felt that I had to persist.

"Apart from jewellery, clothes and furs, are you sure that you have no other substantial assets?"

At this question, Bronia snapped.

"What the hell if I have? They are nothing compared with what Oleg owns." She recovered quickly. "I'm sorry. I must keep my temper under control, but I have a lot of stress at the moment. No, I have no other substantial assets."

Bronia

What I didn't tell Hannah was that I also owned six large apartment blocks in central Moscow, all let and producing a very satisfactory income. These were held in nominee names and dated back to my time in Moscow property before I knew Oleg. He did not know about them and I saw no reason why I should disclose their existence. I felt sure he was going to cheat when it came to disclosing what he owned. I was merely getting my retaliation in first! Whatever I owned, he had fifty times as much.

Hannah

Since Oleg had left, he and Bronia had not talked. She did not know where he was staying but she could contact him through his London office. His current long-term intentions had been made brutally plain by the contents of his petition and the way in which it was served on her but I explained that we had to come to a financial accommodation in the short term. The children were now settled at an expensive private school in London and she was content for the time being to live in the Kensington house. She volunteered to try to make contact with him and see whether he was amenable to a reasonable discussion about short-term maintenance for herself and the children. If not, I explained, it would have to be dealt with through the lawyers and, if no informal compromise could be reached, ultimately by the court, which was likely to be a long, drawn-out and expensive process and might leave her starved of his cash in the present and the immediate future.

I had to explain to Bronia how the English legal system works. We would need to hire a top Queen's Counsel specialising in divorce to represent her in court, who would be supplemented by a more junior barrister to do much of the donkey work. We would also need highly qualified forensic accountants to investigate the complex web of Oleg's assets if, as seemed likely, he was seeking to deny Bronia her rightful share. These would have to be one of the top firms, if only to secure the right international experience. In due course, we would probably need law firms in the countries where the main assets were held to ensure that Bronia received the property awarded to her by the court, unless we could reach agreement with Oleg. At the moment, this looked unlikely but he might soften his attitude in time, especially when he realised how much the fight was costing him. I told her that I would initially answer his lawyers' petition and put my firm on the record in the court. For the moment, I would merely say that we proposed to defend the petition and deny the charges of unreasonable behaviour. Later, we might amend our defence to make our own allegations to seek a divorce but not yet. It was all a question of tactics.

I could see that Bronia was becoming increasingly restive. She was used to getting her own way in a short time frame that she set.

"Why does it all take so long and cost so much?" she exploded. "What's wrong with the legal system in this damned country?"

This was not easy for me to answer. I thought for a moment and replied, "I think you would have similar problems in any developed country with such a complicated property situation."

She seemed mollified and, if I had had any doubts before, I now knew that I had a volatile client who could be calm one moment and fly off the handle the next.

Bronia now changed the subject. "I have a Russian accountant who lives in London and looks after my affairs. I think it would be helpful for you to meet him as he can give you far more detail than I can."

I said that I would be glad to meet him. I thought that it would be helpful to deal with another professional without all the emotional baggage that Bronia brought to the table.

That was enough for the day as I was keen to talk to Sophie and pick her brains about the case. She particularly (and her firm as well) could be ideal in helping me with asset-tracing and recovery. I also wanted her advice on the choice of leading and junior counsel. I had my own ideas here as I practised in the field but not at that exalted level.

Before the staff went home, I needed to check that the rest of the firm was running relatively smoothly. I started with my two new divorce lawyers. There had been an easy transition of my caseload. We had lost a couple of clients who felt that they were being demoted as the boss was no longer handling their work and that was to be expected but in general I was pleased with how well things were going and new clients were still coming in. In fact, the new lawyers were of the calibre to attract clients of their own and I was satisfied that acquiring one huge client was not going to spoil the working of the practice generally by unbalancing it totally.

Sophie

I was very much looking forward to Hannah's call that night. I was realising how much I had missed the closeness of working with my twin, my alter ego, since we agreed to go our separate ways at Cambridge. When she asked me whether my firm and I would be prepared to help on the investigative side, I must say that I was surprised, although on reflection it was perfectly logical. I told Hannah that I would have to clear it with Bill Ramsden in view of her and my incredibly close relationship.

I had been doing my homework on the subject of suitable barristers. Of course, so much would depend on personal chemistry. If Bronia Seratov did not get on with the one chosen, however able and eminent they were, we would need to look elsewhere. On the subject of accountants, there were only about seven firms capable of handling work of this size and complexity. You could be sure that at least one would be conflicted because it already acted for the husband. I felt that Hannah was coping well in this new world in which she found herself.

After we finished talking, I suddenly felt a little flat. Too much living vicariously was not good for me, so I phoned the Agency to organise Sunday night's extracurricular activities. I made a note to myself to call in at the chemist and buy a supply of condoms. Last week's man had forgotten to come prepared and it broke the continuity somewhat to have to tell him to get dressed again and go out to find a chemist in the area that was open late on Sunday night – not an easy task.

13

It Had to Be You

Hannah

I did not at first like Bronia's Russian accountant, Sasha Rubinski, and I was not sure why. It was a gut feeling. He arrived carrying piles of files and account books, accompanied by his mousy, squat little secretary, who was similarly laden. She was giving me filthy looks and I could not imagine what I had done to deserve them. She also insisted on talking to him in Russian, which did not help even though he replied in English.

The atmosphere improved as soon as he dismissed her with an airy wave of his hand. He was perfectly presentable, obviously well-educated and answered all my questions in a satisfactory manner. He was able to give me a detailed analysis of Bronia's financial situation worldwide, including a sketch of what she spent and needed to maintain herself and the children in the luxurious standard which they currently enjoyed. I asked him what he knew about Oleg's finances. He had worked for them both originally until Bronia had poached him to act exclusively for her, so he was not much help on that front as his information was very much out of date, bearing in mind the fast-moving world in which

Oleg operated. As Bronia was taking the children to the family penthouse in Monte Carlo for the weekend, we had to cut short the meeting. Making a concession to possible future penury, she was flying British Airways business class to Nice with the family and a troop of nannies rather than hiring the habitual private jet. What a sacrifice!

I now needed to hire our leading counsel. I had done quite a lot of research already in this area. My everyday clients neither needed nor could afford the top names, so my knowledge at this stage was very much second-hand only. I had Sophie's recommendations and I ploughed through the various legal directories and compiled a list of my top six choices. I did not subscribe to the view that a woman should be represented by a man only, so it was a mixed list as far as the sexes were concerned. I phoned the first chambers and asked to speak to the clerk. As soon as I mentioned my client's name, I was told that his principal could not act as she had already advised the husband. The same thing happened with all six of my top choices. What the hell was going on? I suddenly remembered how easy and inexpensive it was to do what the husband's lawyers had obviously done: send a simple brief to a large number of leading counsel with a little bit of information but no follow-up except subsequently withdrawing the brief, thus compromising the recipients under the strict rules of the Bar so that they could not act for my client, the opponent, on the basis that they were considered to have received privileged information. We were in the realm of exceedingly dirty tricks. They had anticipated which QCs would be approached to act for Bronia and had made sure they would be unavailable by instructing them in this way on Oleg's behalf. If I had had any doubts before that this was going to be a ruthless struggle to the death, they were now removed.

I needed to be more creative and think laterally. I required a Queen's Counsel who above all would relate to and fight for my client. There had to be the appropriate chemistry between them. All the acknowledged leaders at the divorce Bar were out of my reach because of cunningly manufactured conflicts of interests. I had to find someone up-and-coming, extremely able and ambitious who had escaped the conflict net and had not already been briefed on behalf of the husband. I settled on Constance Lasky as my initial choice in the new environment and breathed a sigh of relief when I found that she had not previously acted for Oleg. As a first step, I booked a consultation just for the two of us. While I had been stressing the need for Bronia to be happy with the choice, it was even more important that I would be able to get along with Ms Lasky. There was always a tension between barristers and solicitors, caused by the very nature of the divided profession. At its worst this could lead to a stultifying stalemate and much misunderstanding; at its best the lawyers could spark off each other so that one and one could genuinely make three.

I explained a little about the nature of the client to her clerk. He said he would phone me back. He called fifteen minutes later to say that I was welcome to come round that evening at seven o'clock. The fact that she could fit me in so soon could be a bad sign showing that she was not sufficiently occupied. For the same reason, she could have delayed the meeting to give the impression that she was busy even if she was not. Maybe I was choosing someone who was pleasantly informal and enthusiastic and would make time available despite her busy caseload because she was intrigued and interested. I was soon to find out.

Making my way in on the crowded Central line, I envied those solicitors practising in Central London who could merely walk to their counsel's chambers. I was somewhat frazzled by the time I arrived. I was immediately ushered into a large Gothic-style room with piles of paper everywhere. Constance Lasky was a small, bird-like woman surrounded by a cloud of cigarette smoke who left the shelter of her enormous desk to greet me warmly.

"You need a stiff drink," were her first words to me, "and so do I."

She went to a cupboard in the corner and poured us both two large glasses of whisky without asking me whether I wanted water or ice. As it was, I preferred it neat. There was an imitation coal fire burning in the grate and two huge, rather shabby armchairs in front of it. She sunk down in one and gestured to me to occupy the other. Her Irish accent was very strong.

Reading my thoughts, she announced, "I practised in Dublin for many years before coming over here."

I felt completely at ease and rapidly ran through the important aspects of the case so far. She had a few questions for me, including the identity of those acting for Oleg. When I told her that his QC was Jonathan Fry, she commented, "Yes, it would be he. They don't call him the oligarchs' delight for nothing. Now, it's vital that Bronia gets on well with me. Do you think we will be on the same wavelength?"

We agreed that the only way to find out was to arrange a meeting for as soon as possible. I asked her who she would like to work with as junior counsel. She mentioned Charlie Nicholas, whom I had instructed on a number of occasions and whose paperwork I liked, although we had never actually met.

"He has the right sort of head for figures and facts," she added.

By now, I was feeling very tired and I could see that Constance too was running out of energy. We had both had a hard week. I felt that the luxury of a taxi back to Richmond was called for. Not only could the client well afford it but I was holding plenty of her money out of which to pay for it.

Constance Lasky

Hannah Hoare was not the usual type of divorce solicitor who instructed me. In fact, she was a refreshing change. There was no pretension about her, unlike many with whom I had to deal. I suppose that practising in the suburbs, she was unlikely to have any. In fact, she had a certain humility. I liked the quickness of her mind and obvious fierce loyalty to her client. I thought that I would love to have a solicitor like her representing me if I were getting divorced. She would fight like a tigress to get everything that was due to her client. It was going to be fun working with her. Having not yet met the client, though, I could not be so sure about her. She might well be spoiled and difficult to keep happy. I would soon find out.

Hannah

I thought about the weekend to come. I would have the pleasure of looking after the children but I would have to expend considerable energy in trying to get through to Igor, who was becoming increasingly withdrawn and taciturn. I sometimes felt that I was caring for three children. It would have been nice to put my feet up and enjoy a relaxing time being waited on hand and foot but there was no chance under the present regime. Thank heavens I was still young and energetic. The future might bring other problems but I had no time at present to think too far ahead.

Igor

I would have to have a serious talk with Hannah over the weekend. I had received a more-mysterious-than-usual call from Alexei. He loved the cloak-and-dagger stuff at the best of times but the instructions to meet in an obscure pub in Greenwich, where neither of us was known, seemed over the top even for him. He was already seated in a well-concealed booth at the back when I arrived, with the peak of a large black cap pulled down over his face and wearing huge dark glasses. I noticed that his fingernails were bitten down to the quick and his hands stained yellow with nicotine.

He hissed rather than spoke. "I'm sorry that I have put you and your family in such danger by introducing you to Bronia Seratov."

"What do you mean?" I replied.

"Whoever helps Bronia Seratov is Oleg Seratov's enemy. He is a most dangerous man and you should not take what I am saying lightly."

I assured him that I was taking his words extremely seriously.

"By being seen to help Bronia, I have put myself in great danger. You will not see me for at least six months until things quieten down. I propose to disappear. You should tell your wife to cease acting for Bronia or you and your family will be in great trouble."

True to his word, he stood up and shuffled out via the back exit. I never saw him again. I was left to buy myself another drink and carefully consider his warning. I decided that I had to advise Hannah to drop the case. I knew it would not be easy for her as she had so enthusiastically taken it up and there was a lot of money to be made from it. Also, being English and living in England, she would find it difficult to understand that my fellow countrymen could operate outside the law and in a completely ruthless manner. Having lived for a large part of my life in Russia and being in close touch with the community here, I had no such illusions.

She was obviously exhausted when she came home too late to put the children to bed. I had sung them to sleep as they had early music lessons the next day, and not being able to see them awake upset her. Our discussion did not get off to a good start.

"You have to give up Bronia Seratov as a client," I began.

"What the hell are you talking about? Are you mad?"

"You don't understand. You are putting our whole family in danger if you continue acting for her."

"Where did you get this crazy idea from?"

"It doesn't matter where my information comes from but, believe me, Oleg Seratov is not a man to cross. He is very powerful and completely ruthless. You must stop for the sake of us all."

"You're completely paranoid. We're not living in the Middle

81

Ages in Russia. He can't harm us here in England. We're not savages. Anyway, I'm earning a fortune from the case."

At this point, I lost my temper. "All you think about is money. Isn't the safety of our children more important?"

She stormed out of the room and slammed the door. She was blind to the power and ruthlessness of these oligarchs and what they could do to us. I felt completely impotent and worried for our future.

Hannah

Igor's behaviour was becoming stranger and stranger. Having been partly responsible for originally introducing me to Bronia with great enthusiasm, he now wanted me to give her up as a client. He put forward some cock and bull nonsense about our being in great danger from the wrath of her husband.

"You forget that we are living in a civilised country and not with the barbarians in Russia," I told him. Frankly, I resented his interference at this stage in my practice. He had long ago abandoned any interest in what I did and I would not tolerate his negative attitude now. Besides, I was enjoying the professional challenge of such a large and complex case far too much, as well as the lavish fees it was earning me.

14

Empty Bed Blues

Sophie

Bill Ramsden turned me down. At first I was upset that I would not be working with Hannah on the Seratov case. On reflection, however, I appreciated that our closeness might be seen to rob me of some of my professional objectivity. We also always tried to maintain a balance in the variety of work done in the department and there was already too much of that type of investigative case. I would have to restrict my role to acting as a sounding board and informally second-guessing Hannah generally. I was about to fly out to Hong Kong on a banking fraud action which could occupy me fully for some weeks, so I would not be able to give the personal attention to unravelling the Seratov assets that was required. To delegate the work or pass it on within the department merely defeated the object of the exercise: to be closely involved once again in working with my sister.

Hannah

I need not have worried. Bronia and Constance got along like a house on fire, so much so that I felt almost surplus to requirements. We now had our leading counsel. Bronia had made contact with Oleg but he was not prepared to talk to her about money or at all for that matter. He did say that he wanted to see the children. It was therefore left to me to contact his solicitors, initially to find out what was on offer and to negotiate the best possible interim deal, as well as arranging a timetable for access to the children for Oleg. I made an appointment for an off-the-record meeting. The Central line was much less crowded earlier in the afternoon and I found a seat on the train and was able to work on my papers.

The Lincoln's Inn offices were as grand as I had anticipated. My bald and elderly opponent, one of the doyens of the profession, found it impossible to resist the opportunity to patronise me as the little woman up from the suburbs. I thought of the parable of the town mouse and the country mouse. Frankly, I did not mind if it helped me get what I wanted for my client. He looked like an Ealing Studios version of the successful Inns of Court solicitor in his black jacket, black waistcoat and baggy striped trousers with a gold watch chain strained tight over his ample middle. He was sporting those gold-rimmed half-glasses that most judges seem to wear. We were in a dark mahogany-panelled boardroom with a blazing gas fire, a far cry from my cheap and cheerful meeting room in the suburbs. At least we produced cut flowers daily from one or other of our gardens. The coffee and biscuits provided were first class.

He stood over the fire, warming his large backside.

"It must be a great worry and responsibility for a little firm like yours to handle such a big case." I saw him looking at my wedding ring. "I would have thought that you were happier at home dealing with household affairs rather than involving yourself in such grave and weighty matters."

I ignored it all, water off a duck's back and laid out my client's requirements for interim maintenance for herself and the children and the access she was prepared to allow. I had to be a little subtle to avoid obviously linking one too much with the other.

There was silence for a moment, and then Mr Pomposity uttered the immortal words, "I hear what you say."

Of course you bloody well do, unless you're stone deaf, I was tempted to reply but true to my subservient role I kept demurely silent with my hands clasped in my lap and my eyes looking downwards.

He abruptly left the room, presumably to phone his client. When he came back, he proudly announced, "As an interim measure, my client is prepared to leave your client and the children in the Kensington house and will pay all the expenses relating to it. He will cover the children's school fees and pay generous maintenance for them. They can have free holidays with their mother by prior arrangement in one or other of the homes that he owns, on the understanding that he will not be present. The current possibilities include Monte Carlo, New York, Barbados, Davos and Bali."

The last three were new to me and Bronia had not mentioned them so they were probably new to her as well. Oleg was clearly acquiring additional assets as we spoke. He offered no maintenance for Bronia on the grounds that she possessed sufficient income of her own. He wanted to have the children every other weekend and for part of the holidays. It was all fine in principle, except for the lack of provision for Bronia. Of course, we needed to agree figures. I felt that I had to establish the precedent at this stage that Oleg had to pay something for her by way of maintenance. After all, the discrepancy between their respective incomes was enormous. Just maintaining the household with the appropriate number of servants cost a bomb, even taking into account Oleg's offered contribution. Then again, there was the cost of active security round the clock. There was the ever-present risk of kidnap for the children and this was in no way diminished because their parents had separated. Top oligarchs' children carried a heavy premium in the ransom stakes.

I had worked out very roughly with Sasha Rubinski, the accountant, just how much it would take to keep Bronia and the children in the style to which they had become accustomed. I doubled the figure for the purpose of these negotiations and, after a lot of haggling, came away with an amount which was not too low and at least acknowledged the principle that the wife was entitled to maintenance by paying her something on the record even if it were not really enough. I felt that this concession was on the cards from the start. They were just waiting to see whether I was prepared to tough it out. Ultimately, when we reached a final deal or the court decreed, I hoped that Bronia would be awarded sufficient of the income-producing joint assets to maintain herself so that she would not need maintenance from Oleg as well but we were nowhere near that stage yet.

That was the relatively easy part, I pondered, as I stood squashed together with the other exhausted commuters on the rush hour train back to Ealing. We now had to compile detailed lists of the respective assets and liabilities, income and proposed expenditure following the split. All this would have to be rigorously probed and I expected Oleg to cheat. We were in a different position as Bronia's assets by comparison were few.

Our only available tactic was to inflate as much as possible the cost of maintaining her and the children at the appropriate standard for a leading oligarch's family. As I bandied figures across the table the next day with Sasha, I must say that I was pinching myself when I compared them with my own relatively frugal housekeeping costs.

For the time being, we did not need to bring in the barristers, accountants and valuers. They would be needed when we received Oleg's affidavit and had to pick holes in all the material that he had disclosed. Bronia's disclosure was far simpler, except where we were creatively calculating her future living expenses. I found myself working closely with Sasha and increasingly enjoying the experience. After years of marriage to Igor, I had come to assume that a lack of a sense of humour was a trait to be found in all Russian males. By contrast, Sasha and I would be consumed by fits of laughter as we invented ever more preposterous items of expenditure for Bronia's budget. Ten thousand pounds per year for licensed dog-walkers was one such item, as were mink-lined yoga mats for each member of the family.

The great thing was that we were keeping the client happy. She had met and liked Constance Lasky. The fact that we did not need the QC's involvement at this stage created no problems. There was plenty of action involving Sasha and me and we made sure that we kept Bronia continually in the loop. I was spending all my time on the case and billing weekly. Once Bronia had approved the bill, I was able to transfer the sum from the client account where I held the money. The original sum was much depleted, so I was very pleased when, unlike Oliver Twist asking for more and getting a negative reply, after I requested a top-up, a cheque appeared by courier within the hour. I assumed that Sasha was making his own arrangements for payment with the client, although he may have been on a salary. It was none of my business.

I realised that the nature of my personal practice had changed radically, at least in the short term. Up to now, I had served the needs of multiple clients almost simultaneously, rather like a juggler keeping many balls in the air with the danger that they will all come crashing down at once. Now, by complete contrast, I had the luxury of concentrating all my attention on the affairs of one client. Ultimately, which did I prefer? I would have to delay giving that answer. There would come a time eventually when the Seratov case finished and I had to rethink the nature of my personal practice, unless I was seen to do so well for Bronia that a queue of oligarchs, their spouses and the like beat a regular path to my door.

15

Cheek to Cheek

Hannah

I was surprised when Sasha asked me out for a drink after a particularly gruelling day with columns of intractable figures. I so much thought of myself as married, a mother and a law firm principal that I had overlooked the possibility that a man might still want to get to know me just as a woman. Igor was becoming increasingly withdrawn, especially after our argument over the Seratov case. Sex on Saturday night no longer happened unless I positively and obviously initiated it and sometimes I just could not be bothered. I had grown to appreciate Sasha. We laughed so much together. I said I needed half an hour to make myself presentable and he replied that he would go and get his car.

It was smart, discreet and new. I did not recognise the make but I did recognise that powerful smell of leather from long ago on Shotover Hill. I didn't want to go locally as I was too well known and we might attract comment. Sasha instinctively realised that and we drove to Strand-on-the-Green by the river at Chiswick. The early evening rush had subsided and we found a quiet corner in one of those pubs that line the riverbank.

I asked for a gin and tonic and Sasha, true to type, drank vodka. Despite the fact that we had been working so closely together, we knew very little about each other. Sasha was divorced with a nine-year-old daughter who lived nearby with her mother and he saw her regularly. He showed me her picture: she was a pretty little girl. He had a flat in Kew which was also his office and spent far too much time working. He had won a scholarship from Moscow University, where he had known Bronia, to the London School of Economics as a postgraduate, where he had studied business and accountancy. He had stayed on to qualify as a chartered accountant and was planning to return to Russia when he was recruited by the Seratovs to run the financial side of their UK operation. They had no problems getting him a work permit.

After a couple of years, he had switched, with Oleg's approval, to looking after Bronia's interests worldwide on an exclusive basis. By that time, Oleg needed a whole team of accountants to deal with his affairs. I asked whether the switch had caused any problems now that the principals were at loggerheads. Sasha shrugged his shoulders and said that the dispute had not affected him so far and he hoped that this state of affairs would continue. I told him what Igor had said to me, and his view was that he was being far too dramatic about the situation. We were living in a much more civilised time and place.

The fire was warm and inviting and I found Sasha interesting. A couple of drinks later, I looked at my watch and saw it was well after nine o'clock. Convention demanded that I brought the evening to a close. We walked side by side to Sasha's car in the pub's darkened car park. He opened the door for me and a few moments later I found myself in his arms, kissing him passionately and being kissed back with equal fervour. It seemed the most natural thing. I was so aroused that I could have taken him into me there and then. Did that smell of leather help?

Suddenly my head kicked in. This was a man with whom I had to work on a daily basis. Was it wise to escalate our relationship into one of passion? My body was crying out for him to touch me all over, which he was beginning to do anyway. I was soaking wet and could feel that he was hard and ready for me. My mind made me push myself away from him, though my instinct wanted to pull him closer. I adopted a hearty, jolly-hockey-sticks tone of voice and opened my window to cool down the atmosphere.

"That was very nice but I must be getting home. Thank you for a lovely evening."

I saw him with some difficulty make the effort to calm down. He had good control. I wonder if he realised how much of an effort it was for me too.

He drove me back to Ealing so that I could pick up my car. We arranged to meet at my office at nine the next morning. I was particularly nice to Igor when I got home, though I resisted the temptation to drag him into bed to finish off what Sasha had started.

The next day working together felt surprisingly normal. We made the same light-hearted, silly jokes as we always did as we painstakingly prepared the schedule of means and needs to be attached to Bronia's affidavit. That evening I went home after work.

The next, Sasha asked me back to his flat for dinner. Dinner was forgotten and I gave myself to him completely. Two hours later, I felt utterly drained and satisfied beyond belief. I felt that I would never need sex again. Three nights later, we did it again. What I did find was how out of condition my body was. I had aches and pains in muscles I never knew I had. I resolved to get fit and, perhaps surprisingly, to involve Igor in the process. The more Sasha satisfied me, the better my relationship with Igor became both sexually and in all other ways. There was a gym down the road from our house in Richmond and I took out a joint membership. We also started jogging together in Richmond Park at weekends and on occasional days in the week before work if time allowed.

I needed Sophie's approval not only of Sasha but also of our relationship and the overall shift in dynamics. I recognised that I was at a vulnerable stage in my life. I was a woman approaching middle age with a stale marriage where we took each other for granted and the sexual interest had dwindled away to nearly nothing. I devoted myself almost exclusively to my work and the children. Without being conscious of it, my sense of self-worth had diminished to a point where I was a pushover for the first attractive man to come along. I had no intention of destroying our limping marriage and I wanted the children to grow up with both their parents living together in relative harmony. I had seen too much of broken marriages as a divorce lawyer. The grass was definitely not greener on the other side of the street in that respect.

If I were strong-minded enough, I could have a long-term affair with Sasha and use it to help keep my marriage together. I now realised that a lot of my short temper and impatience with Igor was caused by mere sexual frustration. I was now deeply satisfied, which reflected itself in my overall demeanour and attitude to Igor, as well as a constant rosy glow on my face. Comments were made in the office about how well I looked. It was true to say that our mutual sex life had improved. The new me could keep two men satisfied.

Sophie

What did I think of Sasha? It was difficult to make a snap judgement. One look at Hannah and I could see the source of her new-found happiness. She absolutely radiated sexual satisfaction. I had a pang of envy and, yes, even of lust. For the moment, I wished I had one man who could do that to me rather than a series of faceless male bodies whom I could dominate for my personal gratification. She was obviously madly in love with him but I knew my sister well enough to know that she would not upset the apple cart. Her marriage was safe.

I asked myself the question again: what did I think of Sasha? He was certainly not Igor. In fact, in many ways he was the template for an extramarital affair. He was dashingly handsome, perfectly groomed and well dressed. He was an excellent conversationalist without in any way monopolising things and a particularly good listener. He was obviously anxious to please and make a good impression on Hannah's twin sister. But did I like him? Did I warm to him? I felt that I needed to know him better. In our nightly telephone conversations, Hannah had kept me briefed on the progress of the affair, so meeting Sasha in certain respects was no surprise.

I know what was troubling me: Sasha was just too good to be true. It was almost as if he were the perfect plant, put deliberately in Hannah's way to achieve what he had indeed achieved. He was like one of my 'gentlemen'. He was programmed to please. But was I merely being melodramatic? Suppose I was wrong. How could I upset Hannah when she was obviously so happy? Was I motivated in part by jealousy? I resolved to keep silent about my doubts and fears. I would merely welcome Sasha as Hannah's lover and business collaborator. In other respects, for the time being I would reserve my judgement.

We still had our nightly phone conversations and Hannah kept me informed of the twists and turns of the case. Oleg was proving as tricky as the proverbial waggon-load of monkeys. I tried not to be oversensitive but the intimacy between us seemed to be diminished. I sensed the presence of Sasha in the background.

Then communication suddenly stopped altogether. Hannah was not calling me and she was not accepting my calls. I tried email, text messaging, fax and all the other methods of communication known to mankind without result. The problem was that I was back in Hong Kong on the job and could not get out. I knew Hannah was all right physically as I spoke on the phone to Igor, who reassured me in that respect but I could not probe too much in case I alerted him to other issues. To all intents and purposes, communication between my twin sister and me had ceased, hopefully only for the short term. Had I done anything to offend her? I did not think so. Anyway, that was not how we normally operated. If one of us had given cause for complaint, the other would immediately raise the issue and we would battle it out. I was very worried and very hurt.

16

Do Nothing 'Til You Hear from Me (Concerto for Cootie)

Sophie

I was in the middle of the biggest case of my life so far. I had been seconded to our Hong Kong firm for its duration as they badly needed my particular expertise. We were in court five days a week and preparing for the day or analysing the evidence before and after court and also at the weekends. I made sure I had an hour in the gym early in the morning six days a week and I kept Sunday evenings free. I would book a room in one of those large, busy but rather sleazy hotels in Wan Chai. I had now graduated on a regular basis to two men at a time. It required a knowledge of anatomy as well as acrobatics but the men seemed used to it and my appetite was becoming increasingly voracious. I sometimes worried that I was spoiling myself for a normal relationship with a man. The time ought to come when I would give up my present hectic lifestyle and settle down with a husband to have children and a more natural life but I couldn't see it. Hannah had started out with an ordinary family life and had now taken a lover. Perhaps we would meet somewhere in the middle.

I was so busy that it was difficult for me to focus clearly on the rift with Hannah. Why did she not want to talk to me? What was she trying to hide from me? It had started while I was still in London, just before I left on the current trip. I was also badly missing my contact with Charlotte and Ivan. I had got into the habit of talking to them regularly on the phone when I was away. It had to be something to do with Sasha but what? I phoned our increasingly aged and infirm parents to find out if they knew anything but drew a blank. I had to be careful not to upset them. They looked upon Hannah as some sort of paragon of domestic virtue and worried about my continuing spinster status and frantic, nomadic lifestyle. As things were at the moment, I was the pillar of stability and it was Hannah who was lost out there somewhere in the wilderness.

It had been a typically busy day in court and afterwards, following a lengthy and fraught case conference, I had collapsed at about eleven o'clock on my bed in the Mandarin Hotel without even having the energy to take off my make-up. I could not have been long asleep when I woke up with a scream. I was sweating profusely and shivering at the same time. Something terrible had happened but what? My immediate thought was that it must be Hannah. I phoned her mobile but got no answer. I tried Igor's, with the same result. I called their landline but it just rang and rang. The same when I called Hannah's office. It was still early in the morning in the UK. In desperation, I phoned my London office. Typically, they were already working. My PA sensed the urgency in my voice and promised to phone back as soon as she had any news.

The call came within the hour. There had been a dreadful accident. Hannah and Igor had been jogging early in the morning in Richmond Park. They had both been hit by a vehicle which had not stopped, a hit-and-run driver. Both Hannah and Igor had died instantly. There was no means of softening the impact of such news and to her credit Tracey didn't even try. I thanked her and sat there, too stunned to weep. My immediate thoughts were of the children. I had to be there with them. I phoned down to the hotel concierge. The next available flight was later today in the evening; it was now past midnight in Hong Kong. I phoned our parents and told them the news. I was worried what the shock would do to them but they seemed more or less all right. They were glad I was coming home.

I spent the day sorting things out with the case. Everyone was full of sympathy but I was numb. I packed a small bag. I had no idea how long I would be away but I had plenty of clothes in London. I arrived early at the airport and found a quiet corner in the first-class lounge. I wrapped myself in blankets and took a sleeping pill as soon as I was on board the plane. I didn't want a drink and I had no need of a meal. All I wanted to do was cover my head and try to sleep. I knew I was eventually going to wake up to reality and grief but, please God, not yet.

It was a grey day at Heathrow, which matched my mood. I took a taxi to Richmond. I was greeted by the children and the housekeeper, Claudia. I had not paid much attention to her before. She was middle-aged and rather overweight. I knew that Hannah had relied on her and trusted her implicitly. She was truly part of the family and was suffering as much as the rest of us. The enormity of what had happened now hit me and we cried together. Both children were old enough to at least partly understand, which meant that I did not have to invent some story to cover the situation with them.

"Is Daddy going to come back?" Ivan asked me.

I swallowed hard and wondered how best to handle his question.

"I hope he will soon." I decided that honesty was not the best policy for the time being with him. "I'm here now to be your auntie and take care of you." I was torn between giving them as much comfort as possible and the knowledge that I must not promise what I could not deliver.

Charlotte looked closely at me. "You're not our mummy, though you look very like her. Will you really stay and look after us?"

I was saved from answering by the arrival of my parents, so I had to make a new effort. We all needed help but I did not know where to look for it. My father suddenly remembered his past calling and went into full vicar mode. It was very comforting and I was glad that the responsibility had been taken off me. I felt so lost. I had never had any Christian faith after the age of six. Now to hear my father in full flow was such a consolation. I slept in the spare room that night. I could not even look in Hannah and Igor's bedroom, which my parents occupied. I needed another sleeping pill to put me to sleep.

I knew the next day that I had to try to create a semblance of normality. Claudia got the children ready for school and gave them their breakfast but I drove them to school in what had been Hannah's car. Igor's still had to be collected from where it had been left in Richmond Park. I needed to get closer to the children to try to compensate for the loss of their parents. I already had a head start as their much-travelled and glamorous aunt (I could discount the Russian side of the family), who regularly brought them interesting presents from faraway places. At that point, just when the hard work of looking after them was about to start, I usually made my excuses and left. Things were now very different and I knew that I owed it to Hannah's and Igor's memory to take on as much of the parental role as I could.

I drove to Hannah's office. The atmosphere there was one of total grief and shock. I could not expect anyone to do any work that day, so I sent them all home. I sat in Hannah's office chair and cried until I was empty. I guessed where she kept her personal papers and soon found the key to open the small safe beside her desk which contained them. Hannah's logic was my logic. Her will was where

I expected it to be. I was appointed the sole executrix and guardian of the children. Apart from a few legacies to charity, as Igor was dead too everything was left in trust for the children. The enormity of the task entrusted to me suddenly hit me. How was I, a single woman with an all-consuming career, supposed to bring up two small children and run, or at least run down, a busy legal practice? A short-term answer was obvious even if the long term required more thought. I needed time off from my job.

Bill Ramsden could not have been more understanding and sympathetic. Bad news always travels fast and he knew the whole story in outline, so I did not have to say a word. I came away from meeting him with six months' paid leave of absence.

Bill Ramsden

Poor Sophie. She looked as if she had aged ten years. There were identical twins in my family as well and I understood a little about their special closeness. She had been an incredibly valuable member of the team and I had no hesitation in letting her have all the time off she needed. I had no idea how she was going to manage on the domestic front. To suddenly find yourself as the sole guardian of two small children when up to now you have lived a totally single life is no joke. I hoped she could make the adjustment. I did not envy her. I would have liked to be more helpful but I knew that she had to cope alone. I had had tragic family problems myself but with time to get used to dealing with them. Hers were so shatteringly sudden.

Sophie

Now for the hard part. I spent the weekend with the children and my parents. To be precise, I spent it with four children as my parents reverted as soon as the initial shock had worn off and my father had completed his Pavlovian pastoral role. Claudia had weekends off, so I had to cope alone. I took Charlotte to ballet class on her insistence and left her there. I could see that she was in a caring environment, felt completely comfortable and at home and did not then need me. Ivan's football practice was another matter. Once again, he begged me to take him. I stood freezing on the touchline, cheering loudly with the other parents.

I needed to get used to the idea quickly: I was now a parent whether I liked it or not. I discovered cooking skills that I did not know I had. I know I could have ordered everything online but I preferred now to shop in person, if only because I was not sure what to order and how much of it. Seeing it all on the shelves made it much easier. I went to Waitrose and shopped till I dropped. At least the fridge was stocked for the coming week. I mastered the intricacies of the industrial-size washer/dryer and ironed everything that I thought needed ironing, probably far too much. I lay down on Charlotte's bed between the two children to read them a couple of chapters from a simplified version of one of my own favourite children's books, *The Wind in the Willows*. I was woken by anxious little fingers stroking my face. Lulled by the soporific tone of my own voice, I had dropped off to sleep just when Ratty was rowing Moly back after his first encounter with Mr Toad at Toad Hall. When it came to my own bedtime, I needed no sleeping pill. I was exhausted and slept like a baby. I would never underestimate the work done by a parent again.

17

You'll Never Know

Claudia

I was full of admiration for Sophie. She was clearly a full-time career girl and in no way a natural mother nor cut out for domestic life. What a tragedy! We were all in total shock. But Sophie worked at it and coped. She not only coped but she excelled. I am sure she knew that she could never take the place of the children's parents but she was certainly doing her very best to compensate for their loss. When I came in on Monday, I expected to find chaos. Not a bit of it! Even the dishwasher had been emptied and the contents stacked away. The children were sitting having their breakfast, washed and dressed ready for school. Sophie took the view, rightly in my opinion, that the children's lives should continue with as near a semblance of normality a possible, despite the tragic events that had taken place. Frankly, I had been thinking over the weekend of taking the coward's way out and leaving as I felt it was all too much for me but I now knew that I wanted to stay to help Sophie. I owed it to Igor and Hannah's memory and I loved the children. Some of that love was quickly transferring itself to Sophie.

Sophie

Refreshed by a good night's sleep, I had breakfast with the children and then dropped them off at their schools. Now for Hannah's law firm. Where to start? I sat at her desk and called for the cashier. I could see her do a double take as she looked at her deceased boss' identical twin. The client accounts were in order and there was plenty of money in the firm's office account to keep things running. I then asked the various lawyers to come and see me. Everything was ticking along nicely. There were a lot of work, new clients kept coming in and it looked as if I was the executrix and at least temporary principal of a thriving legal practice. I would have to decide what to do with it.

I deliberately left Angela and Caroline, the two divorce solicitors, to the last. Once again, they were busy with current files. I wanted to know what involvement they had in the Seratov case, which after all was the biggest one ever to hit the firm. The answer was not much and only by giving minor assistance to Hannah in collating and organising documents, as well as sitting behind counsel in less important hearings. Hannah seemed very much to have kept Bronia's case to herself. After I had finished with them, it was time to look at Hannah's filing cabinets. They stood in a neat row on one side of her office. I opened the nearest. It was empty. I tried the next with the same result and so on. They did not contain one single scrap of paper. There were no labels on the fronts either. I called back Angela and Caroline.

I pointed to the filing cabinets and asked, "What did they contain?"

They answered in unison, "The Seratov papers."

I showed them that the cabinets were empty. "Where did the papers go?"

They had no idea. In the cashiers' department, there were records of client's money received, bills delivered and paid and even a small credit balance amounting to hundreds of pounds. It looked as if Hannah had been working on the case up to the day before her death. After that, there was nothing.

Then I thought of Sasha. If he did not know already, he needed to be told of Hannah's horrible death. He should be able to provide some explanation for the missing files. But where would I find him? I had Hannah's handbag with me. She had left it at home when she went for her last and fatal jog. Inside it was a somewhat scruffy address book. Hannah and I shared a distrust of modern technology where our personal affairs were concerned. There was no entry for Sasha but at the back were some rather worn business cards. One of them was his. I tried his mobile. It went straight to voicemail. The landline just rang continually: there was no answerphone. I tried to send an email asking him to contact me urgently. It bounced straight back. Where was everybody and everything associated with Bronia? There was only one address on the card, that of a flat in Kew which was obviously also his office. I had done enough in the office for one day, so I drove to Kew to find out what I could about Sasha.

It was a small, nondescript block of flats, probably built in the '60s. There was no security and I pushed the front door open. Sasha's flat was on the second floor. I rang and knocked but with no response. I looked through the letter box and saw that the parquet floor in the entrance hall was littered with bills and circulars of all kinds. Sasha had not been home to collect his mail for some time.

I had promised to get home in time to read the children their bedtime story. I had left Ratty and Moly in the middle of the river. This time I would try harder not to fall asleep. If I left now and the traffic was light, I would just make it in time.

I did, and managed to outlast the children on this occasion. I picked up Ivan without waking him and tucked him up in his own bed. Claudia had put supper out for me, which I enjoyed very much. I had not realised how hungry I was as I had forgotten to eat lunch. I sat down in front of the television with Hannah's bank statements. I was anticipating being able to keep one eye on the screen while I watched a programme about fashion and at the same time went through some mundane and standard payments in and out. But what was all this? This was no ordinary personal bank account of a suburban solicitor. There were millions washing around in the account! Who the hell was Condor NV? This company, presumably off shore, had paid more than five million dollars into my sister's account in the last three months. Half of it had gone out to what looked like a firm of investment brokers, while the other half was still sitting in the account. As an investigative lawyer, my alarm bells were jangling deafeningly.

I needed two pills before I could sleep that night. I had an appointment with the police the next morning in connection with the joint inquest on Hannah and Igor. Whatever their differences, I grimly thought to myself, as they had lived together, so they had died together. I resolved to say nothing of my disturbing discoveries. It was in the family's interest that the coroner's investigation was as speedy and simple as possible to reach the obvious verdict of accidental death or more likely an open verdict. It was not a branch of the law with which I was familiar.

We met as a concession at what I was now beginning to call my office. The woman inspector and her sergeant were very sympathetic.

"Did your sister have any enemies?"

I answered honestly. "None as far as I was aware."

"Did she have any money worries?"

Only about having too much, I could have answered but did not. "None that I know of."

Did I know of any reason why the coroner should not reach a verdict of accidental death? I was certain of nothing but my suspicions were being aroused that all was not as it seemed. Still, I answered in the negative. The family's good reputation was at this stage more important than having the police swarming over everything and being likely to make a complete mess of their investigation. If anyone was going to do any investigating, it would be me. The rapier was more powerful than the truncheon.

103

18

Messin' Around

Constance Lasky

I was surprised to get a call from Sophie Hoare, poor Hannah's sister. Of course I knew about the tragic deaths. They were in all the papers. Working with Hannah on the Seratov case had started so well. We were completely in tune and equally quick to grasp each other's points. The other side were pursuing a policy of death by litigation. They had us in court all the time on the most ridiculous applications in relation to financial and other matters. Not that we were blameless as we made plenty of our own applications too, many on equally flimsy grounds. Neither of us had time for any other clients. Then suddenly, it all changed. I'm not sure what caused it but we were now disagreeing, sometimes violently, on both strategy and tactics.

Obviously, you do as little as possible to alienate the judge. This case was sufficiently important for the judge to reserve it exclusively to herself, so we knew who we were dealing with, although I do not imagine that she anticipated just how much of her time would be taken up by it. She had become impatient with the lengthy and detailed lists of extravagant future expenses for Mrs Seratov that

Hannah kept on producing. She had indicated quite firmly that she wanted no more of them. In spite of that ruling, Hannah continued to produce new lists for presentation to the court. I could not think of a better way to antagonise the judge. It was almost as if she was doing it deliberately. In a case like this where both parties adopted an entirely adversarial stance, we needed the judge to be sympathetic to us as far as possible.

I felt that what Hannah was doing was not in the client's best interests. I blamed that Russian accountant who was now sitting in on all our meetings. He didn't say much but I felt he was a bad influence. It got worse. We were trying to identify Oleg's assets in advance of the production of his affidavit listing them, as we expected that he would try to conceal a lot. In a meeting with Bronia Seratov, she mentioned that she had heard on the Russian social grapevine that Oleg had acquired a large block of property for redevelopment almost opposite Harrods in Knightsbridge. We did our homework and the usual cloaked ownership pattern had Oleg's fingerprints all over it. The finance for the acquisition came from the London office of a Middle Eastern bank, which we also learned from Bronia was holding a valuable Picasso painting as collateral security. This had been bought recently at a Sotheby's auction in New York for an eight-figure sum, dollars not pounds and was alleged to be the start of a collection of modern art, in which Oleg had recently begun to take an interest.

The fact that this valuable property was on shore was of particular interest when it came to the enforcement of the wife's rights in her share of the family assets. It would be far easier to get her hands on them than some properties in distant countries with unfriendly legal systems. I was therefore very keen that we should investigate the position further but I saw a glance exchanged between Hannah and the Russian accountant.

"No," said Hannah emphatically. "I don't think that is a profitable line of enquiry. Let's drop it."

This was too much for Charlie Nicholas, who was sitting beside me. He went very red in the face and blurted out the words, "Whose side are you on?"

After that, I was hardly surprised to receive a call from Hannah to say that she was withdrawing our instructions, asking for the return of our papers and adding that she was briefing other leading and junior counsel. I was sad, but ultimately not sorry. You cannot continue to do your best when you are at loggerheads with your instructing solicitor. At least my large fee note was paid by return. I told Sophie all this over a very pleasant dinner in the Middle Temple. She was everything her sister had been until the sudden change of character.

Charlie Nicholas

I was the junior barrister being led by Constance Lasky, acting for the wife in the Seratov case. I was used to working with Constance but I had only been instructed previously by Hannah Hoare on minor matters. We had not met before as everything had been done on the phone or on paper. I liked her immediately when we eventually met and felt we were on the same wavelength. These Russian oligarchs go in for litigation in a big way. The petitioner was getting us into court on the smallest pretext. He was trying to kill us with applications in the hope that our client's funds would be exhausted and she would capitulate. But Mrs Seratov was made of sterner stuff. She too was prepared to rush to court on any excuse.

Let me give you a couple of examples. Vassily, Bronia's eight-year-old son, had outgrown his present bike and needed a new one. Bronia asked Oleg to buy it. He refused. Bronia instructed Hannah to write to Oleg's solicitors to demand a new bike or two thousand pounds in lieu. They replied that Oleg would not budge. Bronia instructed Hannah to apply to the court for Oleg to pay two thousand pounds to buy Vassily a new bike. Incidentally, how you can reasonably spend two thousand pounds on a new bike for an eight-year-old escapes me unless it is gold-plated. My new carbon-frame, top-of-the-range mountain bike did not cost much more. Hannah briefed Constance and me to appear before the judge on the application. Oleg's legal team matched ours precisely. The judge ordered Oleg to pay five hundred pounds for the bike with each party paying their own costs. The costs of the application ran into thousands of pounds – all for a five hundred-pound bicycle!

The second example shows even greater stubbornness and stupidity. Oleg was detained over his designated access weekend on business in Ulan Bator or some similar outlandish place. On his return, he asked Bronia to let him have the children the next weekend and to switch the timetable accordingly. She refused. The anticipated letter arrived from Oleg's solicitor, which was followed by Hannah's reply in the negative. We ended up in court again with the usual team of players. This time, the judge refused to make an order and suggested somewhat harshly that the parties grow up, which they showed no inclination to do. This time, several thousands were spent for no result whatsoever.

While all this was going on, we worked as a close-knit team with a few snide remarks thrown in by way of aside about the obduracy and extravagance of our client as well as her hopefully soon-to-be ex-husband. Then for no apparent reason the atmosphere changed completely. Hannah wanted to alter our agreed strategy and tactics entirely.

The judge was clearly getting fed up with the self-indulgence of both parties. It was as if these two Russians were trying to monopolise her court with their trivial and extravagant demands. In my view, if the judge drops a hint, you listen to it. The husband had already stated on the record that the wife and children could stay free of all expenses at any one of his holiday homes. In spite of that, and against our advice, Hannah insisted on putting before the judge a detailed schedule showing the cost of holidays for the family and nannies in hotels and rented villas, including private jets to get there and back, with the demand that the husband pay for it all on top. How stupid can you get? Judge baiting is a sport where there can only ever be one winner, in my view, and it isn't the client. Constance and I talked about it but we could not see that the changes were in the client's best interests. Hannah, stubborn as a mule, would not budge.

I could put this down to sheer stupidity but I suddenly felt that Hannah was actively trying to sabotage her client's case when she refused to allow us to investigate some strong leads concerning a valuable development property in Knightsbridge which we thought the husband owned. This was totally contrary to every ethical principle that we had learned as lawyers: *My client, right or wrong*. It was impossible for us to carry on and Constance and I were talking of removing ourselves from the case but Hannah got in first. She withdrew our instructions. What happens in the law never ceases to surprise me but this was a unique situation so far as I was concerned.

The Judge

I couldn't work out what was going on. This was by no means the first case between super-rich Russians that I had tried and this couple were living up to my expectations. The atmosphere of hatred between them in court was almost palpable. In my private moments of fantasy, I could see them battling it out with lethal weapons in the arena as a gladiatorial contest rather than in my courtroom. The husband's legal representation was what you would expect: the best and smartest that money could buy. The wife's team was a little different. I had had Constance Lasky before me a few times and I liked what I saw. Her years practising in Ireland put her at a disadvantage in terms of seniority in London but she was fast catching up because of her manifest competence.

I had long marked out Charlie Nicholas as a future judge. He had just the kind of head for figures that this case demanded. As a former solicitor myself, I am always interested in who is sitting behind counsel. In this case it was a new face. I get a bit bored with always seeing someone from the so-called magic circle of smart law firms handling big divorce work but here we had someone from the suburbs, Ealing to be precise, where I live. I could see they were working well as a team and keeping their client in the picture. I think the client found our procedure a bit too long-winded. She would rather, Cossack-like, have been charging her husband on her steed, sabre in hand.

Then suddenly, it all changed. This was a case which I had reserved to myself because of its complexity and the multiplicity of applications arising from the hostility of the parties. It was one where a senior judge was required to exercise considerable control to stop it getting out of hand. I had originally given certain guidance, which the wife's team was starting to ignore. Very well! I supplemented my guidance with some firm directions. I was still being ignored by the wife's lawyers. It was almost as if they were trying to upset me; a very stupid thing to do if you ask me. I looked a little closer and saw that her barristers were positively embarrassed by the line they were having to adopt. I understood that their instructions were coming from Ms Hoare and that they were not happy with them. There were flurries of notes being passed back and forth, much tugging of jackets, shaking of heads and grim expressions.

I was not too surprised to hear from my clerk that both barristers had been sacked and I was waiting to hear who was to replace them. Yet another application was due to come before me in a few days and I wanted to know who would be making the wife's case. Things move fast in the world of the oligarchs. I then heard that Ms Hoare's firm were no longer acting and that the application was adjourned so that the new legal team could get up to speed.

Sophie

What sort of outfit was Condor NV, and why was it shovelling vast sums of money into my dead sister's personal account, which was normally used for paying nothing more sinister than the gas bill? I asked Tracey at my office, the one where I was a partner but on leave of absence, to look into it. Condor NV was a company incorporated in the Netherlands Antilles. Its directors were partners in a law firm there and the company had issued bearer shares only, so there was no register of shares to inspect. Even if there had been, it would only have shown some faceless nominees. Needless to say, it filed no accounts. Its beneficial owner could have been the man on the moon for all I knew or could find out. The local lawyers in Curaçao would tell me nothing. They would validly hide behind their professional privilege and duty of client confidentiality. In fact, if they were to do anything else, they would be in deep, deep trouble. The whole web of offshore corporate structures worldwide is based on impenetrable anonymity.

I was seriously worried about all that cash in the account. The obvious explanation was blackmail. But who could my little sister have been so successfully blackmailing for so much and over what nefarious event or events? It made no sense. In any case, I didn't think she was capable of it. I thought I knew her inside out but perhaps I didn't after all.

Next day, I had to see the police once again in connection with the terrible accident. They wanted me to make a site visit, although I couldn't see the point. This time, I met them at the local police station and they drove me to Richmond Park. It was too much for me and I broke down. When I recovered, they showed me what had happened. Hannah and Igor had been jogging at about seven in the morning on the soft verge. They were on the left-hand side of the road, so the traffic was coming from behind them. There was a thick early morning mist and the only other living beings around apart from whoever was in the vehicle at the time were some grazing roe deer. A large and powerful vehicle, probably an SUV, approached them from the rear at speed, swerved onto the soft verge for no obvious reason, though possibly to avoid some animal or other obstruction on the road, collided with them, tossed them up into the air like a charging bull, leaving them both dead and continued on as rapidly as before. The vehicle and its driver had not been traced in spite of all the usual investigations and appeals

There were no witnesses. I could add nothing and they drove me back to Ealing. I was in no mood for work, so I drove to my flat in the Barbican to collect some clothes and other things. The pile of unopened mail in the hall reminded me of the missing Sasha. Was I being melodramatic? Was there a simple, innocent and logical explanation for an increasingly jarring menu of facts?

I got back to Richmond in time to give the children a bath with rubber ducks for each of them and lots of bubbles. Their innocence and simplicity was in such contrast with all the mess and complexity around me. Charlotte seemed to accept me completely. She knew that Mummy and Daddy had gone to Heaven and were not coming back. I was not so sure about Ivan. He had his father's reserve and I found it difficult to draw him out. It could be that he thought too much. He was clearly missing Igor particularly and flew into rages if he did not have his own way. Both Claudia and I were becoming used to being hit by him. We agreed that we would put up with it for the time being in the hope that his anger would subside along with his grief. I had not yet had the courage to tell him that his father was dead but I think he was getting the message anyway.

I was dreading the inquest in case something nasty came out of the woodwork. As it was, the coroner could not have been nicer and swiftly posted an open verdict. I then had to deal with a very angry Claudia.

"It's not good enough. Somebody should pay for this."

Quite understandably, she wanted vengeance. I did my best to calm her down. I had my own reasons for going along with the coroner's verdict. We could not bring back Hannah and Igor and revenge at this point was low on my list of priorities.

With that out of the way, I was free to organise the funerals. Yes, that of Igor as well. His family in Russia showed no interest in participating once they learned that no money was coming their way. Despite my father's calling or perhaps because of it, neither Hannah nor I were remotely religious. I decided on cremation and we had a simple but sad send-off one dark morning at Mortlake Crematorium. My parents were by now too infirm to attend and Claudia helped me look after the children, who stood between us sadly and silently throughout. I was getting to like Claudia more and more, not only for her unquestioning loyalty but also for her manifest competence. I shut Hannah's old office for the day and all the staff attended. There was a sprinkling of clients, local worthies and members of the press. We went off to a nearby pub afterwards which was accustomed to catering for such events. I could not wait for the last person to pay their respects and leave so that I could settle the bill and go home. I was increasingly being submerged in a cloud of nagging doubts and fears.

19

Bury My Body and I Don't Care Where

Sophie

If it was not blackmail, then what was it? I could not see how any suburban solicitor would have a sufficient hold on a client (or anyone else for that matter) to be able to extort millions in such a short space of time but there were unaccounted-for millions in Hannah's bank account. Perhaps as a City worker I was merely being snobbish about the suburbs. I tried to put myself in her place but it was difficult. If I were receiving large sums of dirty money, would I put it in my UK bank account? Never in a thousand years! I would make sure it was held in a numbered account in Switzerland or in an offshore company whose ownership could not be traced: another Condor NV. What madness possessed Hannah to bring that amount of money on shore?

A large sum had gone to brokers. In my capacity as Hannah's executrix, I contacted them and found that the money had been invested in a wide-ranging and diversified portfolio of investments. I was told that Hannah's instructions had been to invest the funds for the long term. Ever more curious: how did Hannah think that she was going to be able to conceal receiving such huge sums from the prying eyes of the Inland Revenue? Then there were money-laundering and professional issues to consider. It was as if Hannah had suddenly become completely reckless. I had brought her office appointments diary home to see if any of the entries gave me a clue. I was getting desperate and there seemed to be a complete absence of leads. Neither Hannah nor I was renowned for the legibility of our handwriting but here the twin thing once again kicked in. We had no difficulty in reading each other's.

I sat there and as I read, I was amazed at the sheer volume of clients and others she saw in the average working day. It must have been exhausting to undergo so many changes of personality, as I knew that each visitor would require a different approach to put them at their ease. I was filled with renewed admiration for how hard my sister must have worked and dedicated herself. But the picture suddenly changed with the arrival on the scene of Bronia Seratov. The days of multiple appointments were over and the pages much clearer.

But what was this? An appointment with a Dr Guy Holland in Harley Street, immediately followed by a lengthy session at the London Clinic, followed in turn by a repeat visit to Dr Holland a few days later. There were then a series of visits to another clinic in Harley Street and more appointments with Dr Holland. After that, these visits all abruptly stopped. I needed to know Dr Holland's speciality and what went on at the clinic in question. A Google search provided the answers. Dr Holland was an eminent oncologist or cancer specialist, while the clinic specialised in chemotherapy for cancer patients. I checked the date of Hannah's last appointment with Dr Holland and realised that it was immediately after that that she had broken off all contact with me.

My investigative technique in my City cases was based on deductive logic. I now applied it. It looked as if Hannah had been suddenly diagnosed with a severe and life-threatening form of cancer. It was treated with a series of chemotherapy sessions, but they did not solve the problem and halt the spread of the disease. At her last appointment with Dr Holland he pronounced her death sentence. I was very upset at my deductions and particularly saddened that my twin sister had not sought to confide in me but had done the opposite by cutting off all communication. I felt strongly that if it had been my diagnosis, I would have rushed to tell her at the outset and share the sadness with her. It just shows that you cannot know how people will behave under great stress, even your identical twin sister. I now needed to get confirmation from Dr Holland.

I phoned him and explained that I was his patient's executrix and also her twin sister. I needed to see him. He was reluctant at first to reveal anything but my professional skills made me very persuasive. Hannah had a rare form of lung cancer which was gradually metastasising into the bones and the brain. She had at most a year to live. She was likely to remain fit, fully able to function and in possession of all her faculties for another three to six months before the inevitable and swift decline set in. It was ironic that her year was cut short by the dreadful accident. Further, as Hannah's identical twin, I had to think of the possibility that I was particularly vulnerable to the same cancer. I put this to Dr Holland but he felt without giving any reason that he should not advise me. He gave me details of a colleague, whom I visited in a state of trepidation.

Two appointments and some tests later, I was reassured that I was not suffering from the same illness as Hannah. It would have been too cruel a fate for Charlotte and Ivan to be deprived of their aunt as well.

I now had an explanation for why Hannah had not taken sensible precautions to conceal the fact that she had received vast sums of money in a short space of time for which she could not account from a faceless company in an offshore tax haven. As I have already said, I was very upset that she had not confided in me and told me details of her condition. Almost certainly she wanted to spare me the lingering pain and grief and that was the reason she had totally broken off contact with me but that was not how I would have expected her to behave. How well did I really know my twin sister? Sooner or later I would have found out about her illness but I was beginning to understand that news of one's terminal condition can cause unexpected variations of behaviour. But I still was no nearer to finding out what she received the money for or who was behind the payments.

Dr Guy Holland

When Sophie Hoare was put through to me and wanted to see me, I was in a professional quandary. Her sister Hannah had been my patient but she was no longer in a position to give her consent to my revealing any information about her case. Sophie was very persuasive but I felt that I needed advice on the ethics of the situation. I phoned the British Medical Association but they were quite useless. According to them, it was entirely up to me, so I agreed to see her. It was uncanny to have my former patient's double sitting before me. As an oncologist, I am used to tragic stories. Hannah's was as bad as any. She had not smoked for many years and then not very much but she was afflicted with a very rare form of lung cancer. She had looked the picture of health as she sat in front of me but she would be dead within the year. I told her sister everything. She then wanted me to take her on as a patient to see if she was suffering from the same condition. As identical twins, it was a reasonable possibility. However, I felt that it was not right for me to have any further involvement especially as my retirement date was fast approaching and I referred her to a younger colleague.

Sophie

Hannah was not due to live long enough to need to explain her actions. I did recognise, I thought, what was in her mind, judging

116

by the way in which she was investing the money. She knew that her life was shortly to come to an end and she wanted to secure the children's financial future. She felt that she could not rely on Igor in that regard. As their father daily retreated further into his depression, such little capacity as a breadwinner that he had diminished still further. He had almost ceased working altogether. I still had no idea of the source of the funds.

Hannah had had the civilised habit of having *The Times* delivered to the house before breakfast. I had continued with it. One memorable morning, there on the front page was the story of a so-far-unidentified man found dead, suspended by a rope round his neck from Hammersmith Bridge with his pockets weighed down with stones. I felt I knew who that man was. I contacted the police and told them my suspicions that their unidentified corpse was the missing Russian accountant, Sasha Rubinski. I had to be careful not to seem to have too much knowledge as I did not want to have them asking me more questions. I posed as an intelligent but interested member of the public. Later that day, his identity was confirmed in the *Evening Standard*. Sasha's death was being treated as a spectacular suicide reminiscent of that of a well-known Italian banker, Roberto Calvi, under Blackfriars Bridge some years before. Calvi's death is still the subject of debate and is now considered to have been murder rather than suicide.

The investigative lawyer in me was unhappy. I was linking in my mind the receipt of large sums of unaccounted-for money, two hit-and-run deaths, a spectacular suicide and strange happenings in relation to a bitter ongoing divorce between a powerful Russian oligarch and his angry wife. I was the first to admit that I could be hopelessly wrong and I needed to be examined for a strong case of paranoia but you have to admit that it was all very suspicious and strange. Could two and two make six?

20

Poor Butterfly

Sophie

I was busy running a thriving suburban law practice and quite enjoying it. One morning, sitting at my desk in the office, I happened to glance in a mirror on the wall and compare my reflection with the photograph of Hannah that I kept on my desk. I was surprised to see how much more I was beginning to resemble her. I had abandoned my smart, City hairstyle for a looser, curlier look. It was so much more practical early in the morning when we had to get the children ready for school. I had also given up my sharp, pinstriped trouser suits in favour of floaty dresses with floral patterns.

I had put the word about that we were now prepared to take on company and commercial work, one of my specialities. It was flooding in. I had to decide whether to continue the practice or dispose of it. If the former, I had to give up my City partnership and I was conscious that my six months' leave of absence was ticking away fast. If I decided to run Hannah's practice on a permanent basis, I could continue to look after Charlotte and Ivan as I'm sure their mother would have wished, which was my inclination as well. If I returned to the City practice and resumed my nomadic life, that would not really be possible and I would have to make other arrangements for them. I loved being with them and I made a point of tailoring my working hours to fit in with their time off school. They were set up for life financially, provided there were no adverse claims on the money. I transferred part of the balance of the funds to the brokers to invest on similar lines to the first tranche. I also set up formal trust arrangements which would run smoothly whatever decision I made about my own life. I'm not sure why but I retained a substantial sum in cash in the safe at home in Richmond as a kind of escape fund in case of emergencies.

I was interviewed by the police about Sasha Rubinski's death. I did not tell them that he was my sister's lover but stressed the fact that they were professional colleagues working closely together on a big case. They volunteered that they thought it was suicide. Who was I to disagree? There were so many loose ends and unexplained events. Where to start? I felt like a kitten trying to unravel a tangled ball of wool. If only I could find an end it would all become clear so easily… or would it? I tried to set down the disparate events on paper and provide linkage between them:

1. *The Seratov divorce:*
   The legal team gets on well.
   The legal team ceases to get on well.
   Instructions withdrawn by Bronia from Hannah but no paper trail.
   Bills sent to her and paid for work done up to a day before Hannah & Igor's deaths.
   Files removed from firm, leaving no papers. Unusual as normally copies of correspondence between solicitor and client, copy bills & working papers retained.
   No receipt for the files. Where did they go? Who took them? How were they removed?
   Small balance of funds still left in firm's client account, giving me excuse to phone Bronia.

2. *Hannah's terminal medical diagnosis:*
   Query the reason for her reckless conduct in receiving unaccounted-for funds in her UK personal account.
3. *The funds received from Condor NV:*
   Why were they paid?
   Who owns Condor?
4. *Hannah & Igor's deaths:*
   Coroner's verdict open, but query?
   Who drove the car and why was he/she not found?
   Where was the car and why was it not found?
5. *Sasha Rubinski:*
   Where was he when I was looking for him to the time his body was discovered?
   Was it suicide?
   If not, who murdered him and why?
   I understand that the original verdict of suicide on Roberto Calvi was later much questioned.

If I wanted to give way to my conspiracy theories, I could find linkages between the various events but there were still some inexplicable gaps which defied logic. How was I going to find the missing pieces of the puzzle? Then again, I could not discount the possibility that it was all a series of unfortunate coincidences. Perhaps the truth was somewhere in the middle. If it was, perhaps not much further investigation would still be required.

The autopsy on Sasha Rubinski came up with no further suspicious evidence and the subsequent coroner's verdict was one of suicide. The deceased was deemed to have weighted his own pockets with large stones in order to hasten his death. Why did he not just jump into the river and drown? It would have been much easier. The chosen method of death was so melodramatic. It was as if a warning or message was being given but by whom and to whom?

I had to screw up my courage to phone Bronia. I found her

number in Hannah's address book and eventually got through to her. She was well protected and I had first to overcome the suspicions of a switchboard operator and no fewer than two personal assistants. I explained that I was Hannah Hoare's sister and executrix who had taken over her practice. Bronia uttered a few perfunctory words of commiseration and condolence. I told her that I was carrying a small balance in the firm's client account which I wished to pay back to her. She gave me an address where I could send a cheque.

I then decided to probe further. I said that I had been intrigued to find no papers or records left in Hannah's office relating to Bronia's divorce and that I ought to know what firm had taken over the case as enquiries might come through to us which should be passed on. She replied that I could search the court records and clearly intended to terminate the conversation abruptly. I got in first, however. I thanked her and rang off.

21

Who Killed Cock Robin?

Sophie

I was getting nowhere with my enquiries. I needed a lucky break and it came when I least expected it. I was alone, quite late, in the office. All the staff had gone and I was about to leave to read the children the next chapter of *The Wind in the Willows* when a rather scruffy envelope was pushed through the letter box, addressed to me in poor handwriting. I ripped it open to find a short note in the same handwriting.

> *First have your car checked thoroughly for bugs. Make sure it is clean. Then meet me at 7pm tomorrow evening beside the tennis courts in Brook Green with your car facing south. I will already be parked in a black Toyota Prius, registration number LJ37CT. Flash your headlights three times and I will join you. Come alone. That's essential.*

It was unsigned.

I wondered about all this cloak-and-dagger stuff. Bearing in mind recent violent events, was I putting myself in danger if I went?

I looked on the internet for companies that swept buildings and cars for bugs, found one on an industrial estate in Turnham Green and resolved to call them first thing in the morning to make an appointment to have the car done. By now, I had sold Hannah's car and was using my little Fiat Topolino, which I much preferred. If I was taking the children anywhere involving a lengthy journey, I used Igor's old VW estate car which I had rescued from Richmond Park.

Not surprisingly, I did not sleep well that night. I eventually dropped off into a deep and troubled sleep between four and five. It was not dreamless. A ghostly and translucent figure with a blurred outline was standing at the foot of the bed. It looked like no one or nothing that I had ever seen before as it alternately flickered and faded. However, the voice that emanated from it was recognisably Hannah's.

Hannah's Apparition

Don't be afraid, Sophie. I don't think they will want to do to you what they did to me. Go to the meeting. Do as you are asked. I went looking for trouble and I got what I deserved. I didn't have long to go anyway because of the cancer. I thought it best not to tell you about it at the time. Perhaps I was wrong. Sorry!

It was a pity about poor Igor. He knew nothing and he wasn't involved. He even warned me and tried to stop me but I stupidly took no notice. Don't talk to me about Sasha. He was a big let-down. He too got what he deserved. How could I be so stupid as to fall in love with him?

Thank you so much for looking after the children. I always knew I could rely on you but I'm sorry that I messed up your great career. If you get out of this unscathed, have nothing more to do with the Russians. They are pure poison. But please go to the meeting.

Sophie

I woke with a start. The sheets and I were wringing wet. I tried to put on paper every word that I had dreamed. It was Hannah's voice, even if not her face and body. Her words seemed to come in a staccato rush. Like most people, I knew that I had dreams but I rarely remembered them. This one was so vivid and remained fresh in my memory. I could think of a hundred and one reasons why I should not go (or at least not go alone) to the rendezvous but Hannah's spirit was urging me to take the chance. I had to go.

My little car registered bug-free. There was hardly room to install one anyway. Brook Green on a Thursday evening seemed a dark and lonely place. I parked behind the black Toyota as instructed and flashed my headlights three times. The Toyota's driver door opened and a small, bundled-up figure got out and came round to my passenger door. I opened it and the figure climbed in. There was a strong smell of cigarette smoke and stale perfume. Neither of us spoke for what seemed a very long time. I could feel my heart beating. *If the worst comes to the worst I'm bigger than she, if indeed it is a woman*, I thought to myself. *I can handle her.*

At this moment, the street light above us decided to go on the blink. It was alternating between half-power and no light at all. If I felt unsettled before, it was far worse now. Inappropriate memories of the film *Gaslight* came into my mind.

"My name is Olga Korova. I was Sasha Rubinski's secretary. I was also his mistress. He promised to marry me. We both worked for Bronia Seratov. What she did not know was that we were also on the payroll of her husband, Oleg. He paid us twice as much as Bronia did. He did not trust her. Our job was to spy on her. To report back to him everything she did or said."

I couldn't hold it in any longer. I had to know, so I interrupted her in full flow even though I did not want to put her off from telling her story.

"What happened to my sister, Hannah? You're the only person who knows. Please tell me now."

"Bronia's people killed her. Your sister betrayed her. I'm afraid for my life and you should be too," she continued. "These are very bad and ruthless people and they will stop at nothing to get what they want or take their revenge. After Oleg took up with a new woman, he wanted to divorce Bronia and our jobs as spies became much more important."

At that moment, there was a violent rustling in the undergrowth beside us on the green and we both jumped out of our skins. It was only a foraging cat or an urban fox but we were already in a finely tuned state of anxiety. When we eventually calmed down and Olga recovered her voice, she carried on.

"Our job suddenly became much more difficult when Bronia took on your sister as her lawyer as we were missing out on a lot of first-hand information. But Bronia herself made it easy for us by introducing Sasha onto the scene and from then on we were once again reporting everything back to Oleg. It was Oleg who instructed Sasha to seduce your sister and 'turn' her. I hated this plan and only agreed when Sasha assured me that it was just part of the job and it would not affect our relationship at all. I met your sister just once when I was carrying files to her for Sasha when he first visited her office. I immediately felt that she was a threat to me. She was so beautiful."

We were still very jumpy and it did not help when a dark car with low lights and two men inside glided slowly past us. Fortunately, they showed no interest in us.

"The first part of the operation went according to plan. Sasha easily seduced your sister. He was then supposed to persuade her to change sides and join us in working secretly for Oleg. He was authorised to offer her almost unlimited money to achieve Oleg's ends. Oleg didn't care how much it cost. He would rather pay any amount of money to your sister to buy her compliance than a single penny to his wife. Although your sister had fallen in love with

Sasha, she stubbornly refused to abandon her client. She said that her professional ethics didn't allow it. Oleg was getting furious. He was used to always getting his own way. I was getting angry too but for a different reason."

She stopped and dabbed at her eyes with a Kleenex. I asked her to explain.

"It was clear to me that Sasha was falling deeply in love with Hannah. He denied it but I could tell. He was using every possible excuse not to be close to me or make love to me and we had terrible quarrels about it."

Now I knew where the money came from. It wasn't blackmail but bribery. However, my sister was behaving as I would have expected by refusing to take the bait. All those years of legal training and professional practice had instilled a sense of right and wrong which was hard to overcome but she clearly had overcome it.

"We were passing all the information to Oleg about the inner workings of Bronia's case but we were still not able to influence events. Then suddenly, it all changed but I don't know why. Hannah was accepting the money and doing everything that she was instructed to do to wreck Bronia's case."

Of course I knew why she had given in and accepted the money. The reason was staring me in the face. If you are under a death sentence, professional ethics suddenly become less important in your list of priorities. The need to provide for her family's future had clearly become all-consuming but I saw no need to enlighten Olga. I allowed her to remain mystified.

"The situation between Sasha and me was eating away at me. I had always kept some of my clothes at his flat but he now demanded that I remove them. That night, in my misery, I drank half a bottle of brandy. I didn't know what I was doing. All I wanted was revenge. I had the number of Bronia's private line and I phoned her. I can't remember exactly what I said but she and two of her sidekicks were with me within half an hour. I blurted out the whole story of her betrayal by Sasha, me and your sister.

After they had gone, I tried to swallow all the sleeping pills in the bathroom cabinet. I no longer wished to live but I only succeeded in making myself very sick. I collapsed in a pool of my own vomit and woke the next morning with the realisation of what I had done. I immediately tried to contact Sasha but he was nowhere to be found. I even tried calling your sister but she knew nothing of his whereabouts. They are both dead because of my jealous stupidity."

I couldn't help asking. "How did Sasha die?"

"I don't know, but I can guess."

She could say no more for the moment but burst into loud sobbing and I did my best to comfort her. Once she had composed herself a little, she continued. "Now you know everything that I know, I'm going to disappear while I can before they come to get me."

I thanked her profusely for what she had told me and she was gone, leaving behind that same smell of cigarette smoke and stale perfume. I sat there for some time, trying to comprehend the horror of the whole story. I needed more time for it to sink in. I required urgently to address my own situation, and that of Charlotte and Ivan. How real were the threats against us? Who were our enemies and what were they likely to do? I never expected to see or hear from Olga again.

Clearly, Bronia Seratov was a very dangerous woman to cross. Two people had died so far for betraying her, plus one who just happened to be in the wrong place at the wrong time. Had my enquiries made me a target?

Looking back at the story that Olga had told me, I still found it difficult to believe that Hannah had accepted Oleg's ill-gotten millions, which he would rather pay to her than to his wife, in return for 'throwing the fight' like a corrupt boxer taking a dive. She had been told that she had a fatal cancer and only a short time to live and make provision for her children. Her maternal instincts were stronger than her professional ethics. I wondered how I would have acted faced with the same circumstances. I had already compromised my own professional position by failing to disclose to the Inland Revenue the funds received from Condor NV and I could yet do worse. Clearly, once Bronia found out about Hannah's treachery she arranged for her goons to raid Hannah's office and remove all her files and papers. Breaking and entering while leaving no traces were obviously everyday practices for her people. It was unimportant in the scheme of things but I still wondered if the removal of the papers took place before or after the murders of Hannah and Igor.

I had sat in the car far too long, feverishly going through events in my mind. It was time to go home. I started the car and turned right into Hammersmith Road and was approaching the large roundabout at Hammersmith Broadway. I pulled over to allow a police car with blue lights flashing and siren blaring to pass. As I gradually got nearer in backed-up traffic, there were many more blue lights. By the side of the road there was the crumpled wreck of a black Toyota Prius. I could see enough of the number plate to be quite sure that it was Olga's car. Firemen were still aiming hoses at the smouldering wreckage and paramedics were carrying a lifeless body on a shrouded stretcher to a waiting ambulance.

As I slowly drove by, I was wondering whether Bronia or Oleg was responsible for Olga's death. I reckoned that the male of the species could be as ruthless and vengeful as the female in the oligarchs' world. Bronia had no current reason to harm Olga as she had recently helped her so much. It was true that Olga had been her enemy and a traitor to her in the past but Oleg certainly had urgent and pressing reasons to kill her, if only to show others in his employ what happened to those who betrayed him. I could see no sign of any other vehicle being involved. To my untutored but suspicious eye, it looked like the result of a car bomb, although I felt quite sure that a more innocent explanation would be forthcoming from the authorities: an electrical fault, for example. How ironic it was that Olga had warned me of the danger of my car being bugged but had overlooked the risk of a bomb being attached to the underside of her own car. I was cynical enough to think that the incident would be made to look like an accident so far as any investigation was concerned and that the police, in their naivety or their anxiety to avoid extra work, would accept that that was what it was.

22

The Devil and the Deep Blue Sea

Sophie

I was obviously in great danger but from which side or perhaps both? I was fairly sure that I was in a situation where I would not be given the benefit of much doubt. Paranoia, self-preservation, revenge and complete ruthlessness were strong elements in the make-up of both Bronia and Oleg. If Bronia had been responsible for the killings of Hannah, Igor and Sasha, then Oleg had very likely ordered the elimination of Olga, though I could not completely discount the possibility that she was on Bronia's shopping list for disposal as well. Any idea that the deaths were accidental had long flown out of the window so far as I was concerned. I felt sorry for Hannah being duped by Sasha even if he did eventually fall in love with her. I never considered my sister as vulnerable and needy but this proved I did not know her as well as I thought. There was the minor mystery of Sasha's whereabouts from the time of Hannah and Igor's deaths until he was found hanging under Hammersmith Bridge. Either he was held throughout at Bronia's mercy until the final disposal or he was on the run until she caught up with him. I thought the former explanation was more likely. It was true that the inquest showed nothing suspicious but I was sure that Russian torturers could operate leaving no traces. If Sasha had got away, I thought it likely that he would have fled very far, much further than Hammersmith Bridge, knowing what fate awaited him if Bronia caught up with him. I doubted that I would ever know the answer for sure.

These oligarchs had an uncanny way of knowing what was going on. Olga had insisted on my making sure that my car was bug-free. How about my office and my home? I reckoned that it was too late now to do anything about it. Any damage was already done. Oleg was unlikely to be my friend because of my knowledge of the source of the Condor funds and his attempt to subvert Bronia's legal case. I could not prove his involvement in Olga's death; nor, I suspected, could anyone else. Bronia seemed likely to have much more blood on her hands to date and I possessed the circumstantial evidence with a motive to link three deaths which would interest the authorities in pursuing matters further to her considerable discomfort.

On balance, I felt she was the greater danger to me. How about the children? Were they in danger too? Would they take them hostage to get at me or would they murder them too? I thought about going to the police but I did not think that they would take the threat against our lives seriously. After all, I had gone out of my way previously to paint a picture that everything was normal. Suddenly changing tack completely would seem like incipient hysteria and I felt that I was unlikely to be believed. By the time they had investigated and taken any action to protect us, in all probability it would be too late. I reckoned I was out on my own.

I was still in much doubt as to how dangerous our position was when I arrived home. Charlotte was waiting for me with *The Wind in the Willows* open at the page where we had left off last time.

"Can we have the finish now?"

Ivan was looking at me with a strange expression that I couldn't read, as if he knew something that I did not. I was aware that good was going to triumph over evil in the final pages of the book and wished I felt as confident of a similar conclusion in our own situation. I read to the end and then tucked them up for the night in their room.

I did not have much appetite but managed to eat what Claudia had left out for me. Then I decided to put together an escape kit. I found a small rucksack in a cupboard and filled it with our passports, the children's birth certificates, Hannah and Igor's death certificates and a copy of Hannah's will and probate which showed me as executrix and guardian of the children. Igor left no will or property of his own. I did not want some jobsworth at a border questioning my right to be in charge of the children and accusing me of abducting them. I included all my credit and debit cards, together with the considerable sum of cash that I had kept in the house. Lastly, I added a wedding photograph of Hannah and Igor. I put out my clothes and the children's for the next day and, on impulse, re-parked Igor's car in the mews behind the house, leaving mine on the drive at the front.

I was still not convinced that I had anything immediately to fear but I did go to bed with a troubled mind and a glass of whisky and hot milk. They did not stop me from dreaming vividly – Hannah's ghost, if that was what it was, stood shimmering once again at the foot of the bed. This time she was surrounded by wisps of what looked like smoke or fog, which were getting progressively thicker. Again, it was Hannah's voice, but from far away.

Hannah's Apparition

I'm so sorry, Sophie. What a mess I've got you into. If only I hadn't been so damned ambitious. Bronia Seratov was out of my league. I should have known it. I should have turned her down as a client. As for falling for that little crook, Sasha Rubinski... I feel ashamed. I think you understand about the money. I wasn't interested for me. I told Sasha so again and again. I wouldn't take it. It was only when the doctor gave me my death sentence that I weakened. Cancer changed everything. I knew that Igor could not provide for Charlotte and Ivan and here was a big chance to secure their financial future after I had gone. I probably should have been rock solid and stood by my professional duty. Frankly, by now I had grown to hate and despise Bronia as a cold, money-grubbing, ruthless, dishonest, using bitch. I wanted to damage her. She was no better than her husband. These oligarchs are heartless crooks who have raped their country and its people. They will make use of anybody, drain them dry and then discard them. I couldn't care less whether she adds a few more millions or billions to what she has already or loses the lot.

Don't underestimate either of them. You are in great danger. You should all get out while you can. Please continue to love and look after the children as you have done since I died. I'm sad that I wrecked your wonderful career. I know it's not much consolation but I would have done the same for you in looking after your children, as you well know. These Russians are animals.

Her faint voice suddenly strengthened to a scream.

Go now. Get the children. Run!

Sophie

I woke with a shock and my heart racing but with renewed courage also. Fingers of white smoke were curling under my bedroom door. I could smell an odour of scorching somewhere. I opened the door and saw in the hall below that the smoke was getting thicker at ankle height and drifting in patches at knee height but still with occasional clear gaps. In one of the gaps I could now see the source of the smoke.

There on the doormat just inside the front door, obviously pushed through the letter box, was a cylindrical-shaped silver object with one end glowing like a cigar and from which the smoke was escaping intermittently. My father had often entertained us with lurid details about his time in the ARP during the war and I knew an incendiary bomb when I saw one. It was only a question of time before it exploded and flames erupted.

All this seemed to be happening in slow motion but in reality it only took panicked seconds. I threw on my clothes, woke the children, protesting, from their deep sleep, dressed them hurriedly, grabbed the rucksack and shepherded them out of the back door to Igor's waiting car as the smoke grew progressively thicker and reached well above waist height. I drove as fast as I could straight to Terminal Five at Heathrow as we all still coughed and spluttered.

The British Airways ticket office was just opening and I bought three economy tickets on the first available flight. It happened to be to Paris but I didn't care where we were going as long as we got away and got out of England. I changed a wad of notes into Euros, then phoned home in the hope that it was still standing and the fire was yet to become uncontrollable, as I wanted to ask Claudia, who should have arrived at the house by now, to tell the children's school that I had taken them away on a trip. There was no reply. She had had her mobile phone stolen the week before and hadn't yet replaced it so I had no means of getting in touch with her. I wondered whether the house was still there or consumed by flames by now. I hoped that Claudia was all right. I breathed a prayer of thanks as the plane took off but felt that our troubled journey was only beginning.

23

Around the World in Eighty Days

Sophie

I looked for the quietest corner in the departure lounge for the three of us. I felt that we needed to be as inconspicuous as possible. I was sure that Bronia's spies had been watching the front of the house. Luckily, nobody had seen us at the back or at least we had seen nobody there. They probably assumed that we had been burned to ashes as we slept in our beds. Nevertheless, we needed to be on the watch and I had a feeling that I would never be able to relax again.

I was trying not to alarm the children but it wasn't easy. I told them that we were going on a great adventure but my agitated behaviour contrasted with my encouraging words. They were perfectly happy, at least for the moment, as they had their cuddly toys to look after. I took the opportunity to leave a voicemail message on Bill Ramsden's office phone. I did not want to speak to him as it would have been so difficult to answer the inevitable questions. I said that I was resigning from the partnership with immediate effect and I hoped one day to give him an explanation for my seemingly extraordinary conduct. I thanked him for all his support during my time with the firm.

I was in a dilemma as to what to do about the Ealing practice. I wished now that I had taken the immediate decision as Hannah's executrix to dispose of it. I reckoned that a few days would pass before the firefighters realised that the children and I had not been consumed by the fire. I was sure that Bronia's people (and I was almost certain that it was her gang rather than Oleg's which was responsible) had done a most efficient job and destroyed the house completely. Fortunately it was detached and I hoped that the neighbours had not suffered also. I anticipated that the wreckage would take some time to cool down before a proper search for our remains could be carried out. I decided to take no action regarding the practice for the time being. Frankly there was nobody I could ask to deal with the problem. I realised how lucky Hannah was to have had me. It was only a question of time before Bronia knew that we had not perished in the fire and were on the run. She was bound to come looking for us with all the plentiful resources available to her.

We boarded the flight and took our seats. I could not stop turning round to scan my fellow passengers in case, despite the likelihood of our deaths by fire, one of Bronia's agents had followed us after all and was on board. The rational part of me appreciated that I was very unlikely to recognise any such agent but at this time I was filled with all sorts of conflicting thoughts and emotions and not thinking rationally. The children by now were asking questions.

"Why was the house full of smoke?" was Charlotte's first query.

"Because a fire had started," was my lame reply.

"How did that happen?" Ivan joined in.

"I really don't know. I think it was an accident," was the best I could manage.

"Where are we going?" they asked in unison.

"On a magical mystery tour." That one was easy.

"When are we going back?" It was Ivan's turn to ask the difficult question.

"You'll have to wait and see."

We landed at Charles de Gaulle Airport and took a taxi to the Left Bank. I found a small hotel off the Rue Jacob which had a large room with three beds in it. We needed to do some shopping as we had left the house with only the clothes we were wearing. It was easy to buy what we needed, together with toiletries and a cheap wheelie case in which to put them. We were now on the run and I had to devise some sort of strategy to try to keep us ahead of our pursuers.

Clearly, it was not safe to stay too long in any one place. I did not underestimate the power of our adversaries. I expected them to have unlimited personnel as watchers everywhere we might go. I was also concerned that they might have access to official passport data, airline passenger lists and credit and debit card information. It was fortunate that I had a lot of cash to burn through before I needed to resort to cards. I would put that day off as long as possible.

We were of course now in the Schengen zone of the European Union. If we stayed in it, there would be no need to produce our passports when we crossed borders. This could be a great help in avoiding discovery. I toyed with the idea of using my professional contacts and clients in Europe to smooth our path but reluctantly decided that it was better to avoid them all. There would be too many questions asked which I couldn't or didn't wish to answer. News of where we were could get back to all sorts of people and there was always the risk that it would reach our enemies. I was mixing caution and paranoia in equal proportions.

I had taken the children out of school without notice. Despite the fact that we were trying to avoid pursuit I could still try to improve their general education. That afternoon we visited the Louvre. Over the next few days, we saw many other tourist sights.

137

I estimated that we were as safe concealed among the hordes of tourists as we would be anywhere else.

Our notional three-day 'honeymoon' had come to an end. By now it would be known that we had not died in the fire. I bought all the English newspapers every day. On the second day, I found a short paragraph about an as yet unexplained fire which had destroyed a house in Richmond, Surrey, with the seeming loss of the sleeping inhabitants, an unnamed adult and two young children. I found no other reference. I was strongly tempted to contact Tracey to find out more news but I reckoned that it was unfair to make use of the services of a firm from which I had resigned so precipitately. There was also the risk that they, whoever 'they' were, were expecting such a move and tapping the firm's phones. I discounted no possibility at that stage. It was far safer to cut off all communication.

I thought of contacting my parents to let them know that their surviving daughter and grandchildren were well but any enemy would anticipate that such an approach would be made and would be looking out for it. In other words, their phone was likely to be bugged and anyway, what had happened would be far too difficult for my parents to grasp at their age. With a heavy heart, I decided that it was better to say nothing. They would learn that we had not died in the fire. That had to be enough for the moment. I hoped that we could survive and reconnect with them before it was too late. They were not going to live forever.

We took the TGV to Nice. The children thought it was a great adventure. I shepherded them away from the rather menacing atmosphere around the station and we took a room in a small hotel behind the Promenade des Anglais. It was now warm enough not only to walk on the beach but to sit on it. I bought the children plastic buckets and spades in lurid colours and all sorts of shapes. I enjoyed playing with them just as much as the children did. However, after a four-night stay I reckoned it was time to move on. I felt we were less likely to be noticed and discovered in a busy city, so I chose Barcelona as our next stop. There was a train leaving early the next morning and the children liked the idea of visiting a different country. I bought them each a sticker book in which to put the flags of all the nations that we were going to visit on our magical mystery tour.

In an estate agent's window, I found a small apartment available for a short let of a week. This apartment had the advantage of its own kitchen. Eating at home was a nice change from restaurants and much less public. Frankly, we were tired of eating out all the time. Then again, the sight of two English children in Spain and not in school during term time might cause adverse comment. The more we kept out of the public eye, the better. In a good bookshop I found some reading books in English appropriate to the children's ages and from then on I devoted at least an hour a day to reading with each of them. I wanted to inject as much normality into their itinerant lives as possible and I viewed schoolwork as a priority. I was keeping an eye open for books in English on other school subjects but I found nothing further in Barcelona. The children were fascinated by Gaudi's cathedral, La Sagrada Família and the ongoing work to complete it. I comforted myself that I was giving them the equivalent of the grand tour that young English aristocrats used to undergo but in the case of the children at much earlier ages.

When our week was up, we moved on to Madrid. The children loved all the art in the museums and I watched their jaws drop when they first encountered the works of Picasso. Once again, we found a tiny apartment for a week. I was still very much aware and on my guard but I was generally becoming more confident that we were not being closely pursued. Travelling by train left less of a footprint, so I generally chose it over flying where passports would have had to be produced.

We then went back to Paris and took a flat in Montmartre. We were beginning to think of Paris as home but that could be dangerous. Anything likely to lead to a pattern and complacency had to be avoided. I managed to find some second-hand maths and geography books in English on one of the stalls by the Seine, so I could widen the children's curriculum. I told Charlotte how good her mother had been at mathematics and challenged her to do better.

The question of what the children should now call me came up quite naturally in conversation. In fact, Charlotte raised the issue. They had graduated from 'Auntie Sophie' to 'Sophie' and now they both spontaneously suggested that in future they should call me 'Mum'. I was very moved and also flattered and had to wipe away a tear. I think they somehow instinctively knew we were on the run and 'Mum' would avoid awkward questions being asked. It also reflected the fact that, to all intents and purposes, that's what I was and was likely to continue to be.

We moved on to Belgium and then Holland, continuing to traverse the Schengen zone by our preferred trains and buses. I was pleased that the children took it for granted that we would visit the museums and art galleries in every city that we found ourselves. They were developing a lively curiosity and never seemed to be bored. I wished that I had had the opportunity to learn so much by this method when I was their age, though without the underlying pressure of our flight.

Now it was time to visit Italy. It was a long and convoluted journey by train with several changes. The train terminated at Rome, so that became our destination. There are many small and discreet hotels near the terminus and I chose one of them. It took at least a day to recover from the journey before we were ready to start sightseeing. I viewed our stay in Rome as a wonderful chance to further the children's education. This was truly learning by travelling.

After a heavy morning traipsing around the Forum, guidebook in hand, we were relaxing over enormous ice creams in an outdoor café in the Piazza Navona, watching the sunlight playing on the water spraying over the intricately entwined group in one of Bernini's fountains, when I noticed a man at another table somewhat obviously taking an interest in us. My internal alarm bells started jangling loudly. My initial reaction was to pay the bill quickly and get out of there but it was too late. He was rising from his seat and walking towards us with something of a limp. He was not a very prepossessing figure. In fact, he reminded me of Peter Lorre in the classic film *The Maltese Falcon*. He was short, slight, shabby and unshaven. As he approached us, he was looking around him as if he were worried whom he might see or be seen by. *I know that feeling*, I thought.

"Aren't you Hannah, Igor Zabrinski's wife?" he hissed. "He's a friend of mine and he often showed me photos of you and the children. I'm Alexei. Doesn't he talk about me sometimes? I used to sell kitchen goods at a discount to some of his friends and do other deals for them."

I swallowed hard. This was all far too close for comfort. It could be an elaborate ploy by one of the agents of Bronia or Oleg to entrap us. By talking about Hannah and Igor as though they were still alive, he may have been trying to allay our fears and lull us into a false sense of security. He was such a shifty-looking character, I instinctively felt that he could not be trusted. Even if he genuinely thought that Hannah and Igor were still alive, he could easily soon learn the truth and he looked as if he would be all too ready to sell information about us to the highest bidder. What was he doing in Rome anyway? Did I believe in coincidence? This was not an auspicious beginning.

I managed to clear my constricted throat. There was no point in denying at this stage that I was the person he thought I was, even though I was not. It was not the first time that I had impersonated or been mistaken for Hannah or she me.

"Yes," I replied, "he often talks about you. This is Charlotte and Ivan. I have taken them out of school for a few days so that they can learn about ancient Rome."

As I talked, I was thinking quickly that if Alexei was not

141

currently the agent of Bronia or Oleg, meeting us gave him the ideal opportunity to ingratiate himself with one or the other by informing them of our current whereabouts as well as earning a substantial reward for the information. My paranoia was working overtime.

We were suddenly saved by Ivan. "I need a wee," he announced loudly.

"Yes, dear," I replied, "I'll take you in a moment when I've finished talking to this gentleman."

"No, I need a wee now!" He shouted, going purple in the face and stamping his foot.

I made my apologies to Alexei, gathered up both children and my handbag and made for the toilets in the café behind. We left our raincoats and Alexei to pay the bill but I had no intention of going back. The situation was far too dangerous. We could always buy new raincoats but once captured, could not easily purchase our freedom again. After Ivan had relieved himself, we found a door at the back which opened onto a filthy alley crammed with tall and evil-smelling refuse bins. There were rats scurrying around enjoying the overspill of the rubbish but we were in a panicked flight and hardly noticed. We zigzagged up and down a few streets and alleys until I saw – blessed relief – the light on an unoccupied taxi. We took it to the Piazza della Repubblica and then switched to another taxi back to our hotel. I was taking no chances, and remembered some of these tactics to avoid surveillance that we used to see in old B-movies.

We arrived back at our room very shaken and it took us all some time to calm down. We needed to get out of Rome as soon as possible and I went down to the front desk to borrow a train timetable.

It was only when we were on the night train to Milan that I was able to relax and review what had happened. The chances were that Alexei was genuine and, as he was away and out of touch, did not know of the tragic deaths of Hannah and Igor. I knew from experience that it is a lonely business being on the run and friendless, as he seemed to be. Seeing what he thought was a friendly face that he recognised in a non-threatening atmosphere, he dropped his guard and approached us. Then again, even if that were true, Alexei had told me of his reputation as a wheeler-dealer. Just as he sold household appliances, he could sell us when he got more information and discovered that we were on an oligarch's wanted list. I still could not discount the converse proposition that he was now in the pay of one of our enemies and it was all a set-up. I might never know the answer for sure.

I resolved to be doubly careful in future. We moved cities every three or four days and the nomadic life was becoming exhausting. We started talking of finding a remote place to settle down. This would be in direct contrast to our previous decision to hug the big cities where we could more easily seek anonymity.

We arrived in Munich on an overnight train, tired, cross and dirty. We fell into a dump of a hotel near the station. We just didn't have the energy to look for anything further and better. All our clothes were crumpled and filthy. We had had enough. We now needed to implement those plans to settle down but I did not think that Germany was the place for us. After a few days to recover, I booked easyJet flights to Pisa. I initially suggested the train but the children rebelled. They had had enough of trains and I sympathised with them. I thought that Italy might be the country where we could establish a home. I had always loved the language, the scenery, the people and the food.

We arrived in good spirits and I rented a car. I knew I was taking a risk as the hire company took my passport and credit card details but I comforted myself with the thought that there are many rental companies and no central register. Anyway, I had already broken my previous rule by flying rather than using the train, so our details were on record as it was. I would not have been so relaxed about these issues in the earlier part of our trip but I felt that so much time had now passed that the danger to us must be receding and that the heat was off.

For the next few weeks we toured Tuscany. We spent time in all the big towns and a number of smaller ones and villages as well. As it was out of season there were some amazing bargains available. We stayed in everything from luxury hotels to crumbling Palladian palazzi. I knew I was searching for something but I was not quite sure what it was. We had been renting a seaside villa at Porto Ercole on the Monte Argentario peninsula and were heading north in the general direction of Siena along the Via Aurelia. I planned for us to have lunch in Grosseto but I could not find the centre as the road signs were so confusing and we became trapped in the dreary suburbs. I decided to continue the journey. On an impulse, a road into the hills looked attractive and it started to climb and wind. We were all very tired and hungry by now. I drove on, drawn by the tree-covered hills in contrast to the flatness of the Maremma plain which we had just left behind.

We rounded a bend and there it was. Bathed in sunlight was the perfect Italian village. Perched on a large rock with the tip sticking up in the middle, a castellated clock tower at one end and the ancient church at the other, its houses seemingly piled on top of each other, it looked a little like the Rock of Gibraltar. The car almost seemed to find its own way into the centre of the less attractive lower village. The more beautiful medieval upper village loomed above us. A neon sign indicated the Trattoria da Sole. It looked open. We got out of the car, tired, hungry and stiff and made for the welcoming entrance.

24

The Folks Who Live on the Hill

Sophie

As I have already said, we spent a very pleasant number of months in the village. The children enjoyed the local school and made new friends. Their Italian started to be better than mine and was certainly more colloquial. I had told Enrico, the estate agent, that I wanted peace and quiet to write and indeed I started to put down on paper the extraordinary story so far involving my late twin sister Hannah and myself. I was wondering what more there could possibly be to write. The initial panic had passed and I was viewing our future with growing confidence. Perhaps all the excitement was over and we were due a time of undisturbed tranquillity.

If the weather had been like this when we first arrived, we would never have found the village at all, shrouded as it was in a dark, unmoving, cold, clammy cloud. Even if we had discovered it by complete chance, the place would have seemed so unattractive and unwelcoming that we would have immediately moved on. The locals talked to me about the *nebbia* or fog, which you could almost cut with a knife. After all, the weather was the regular topic of conversation together with football but this was our first experience of the fog and I didn't like it. The village was 580 metres above sea level and our house was at the very top. In the winter, our biggest problem was with the wind. The house was north-facing and sometimes it was difficult to close the front door because of the force of the wind beating against it.

That day, there was not a breath of it and it seemed unlikely that there would be any change for a considerable time. The problem was that a low cloud had become 'hooked' on the tip of the rock and the village was in effect lost in it. The lower village was less affected as the cloud was not so thick there. The higher you climbed, the worse it got. Here at the summit you could hardly see your hand if you extended it in front of your face. What made it worse was the cold, the eerie silence and the moisture that seemed to drip everywhere.

There was no school today and the three of us had been out in the lower village doing our shopping. It was not a day for the outdoors and we returned home, glad of the comforts of central heating, thick stone walls and tiled floors thickly carpeted with Persian rugs. After the children had helped me clear away our late lunch, we settled down at the kitchen table. I was reading a primer to improve my Italian syntax while Charlotte and Ivan were absorbed with crayons and their colouring books. I got up to look out of the window and saw that it was now completely dark. We could have been adrift in outer space and there seemed to be no context to our existence. I closed the inner shutters and lowered the heating as it was actually getting too warm in the house.

I had just about got back into my book when I paused, startled. There were heavy footsteps outside. People were walking slowly and purposefully but silently around the house as though they were

146

exploring its exterior and making no attempt at concealment. The sound faded away and I waited to hear if the footsteps resumed at the rear. I told the children to be quiet and switched off the lights. I was still hoping that I would hear nothing more and that the footsteps were not sinister but now I heard them again at the back. They had caught up with us!

I had designated the cupboard under the stairs as our place of refuge if they found us and I now scooped up the children and dashed for it. I pulled the flimsy door to and we lay huddled together on the cushions I had previously placed there with our hearts beating fast waiting for the next sounds.

We did not have long to wait as there was a splintering crash of wood as they jemmied open the shutters on the back terrace. I had always recognised this as our weak point. This was instantly followed by the sound of breaking glass as they got through the inner door and opened it by the handle from the inside. They were now within the house.

I paused to think who 'they' could be. They were either Bronia's or Oleg's men. Neither of them were likely to show us any mercy. I could hear heavy boots cautiously exploring the rabbit warren of rooms upstairs. Clearly they had not switched on the lights and were either working in the dark or by flashlight. I pulled the children closer to me and could feel the trembling in their little bodies, like two puppies. I doubted that I was shaking any less from fear. I was concentrating on keeping our heads down but I knew it was only a question of time before we were discovered. Theirs was a methodical search.

The sound of an explosion at the front door interrupted the footsteps and we could hear more heavy feet rushing in. Acrid smoke swiftly filled our hiding place, leaving us coughing and spluttering. The new group were now locked in combat with the first one. There was the phut-phut sound of silenced firearms which I recognised from the movies, together with strange cries and groans. It was all over very quickly, followed by silence but once again I heard the sound of heavy feet cautiously approaching.

Suddenly our door was violently wrenched open and we were blinded by powerful flashlights. Rough hands grasped us and carried us outside with as little effort as if we were bundles of dirty washing.

We stood trembling on the front terrace, still blinded by the glare. Gradually our vision cleared but I was not encouraged by what I saw. Three men were scrutinising us intently. All three were dressed in black commando-style clothing. The two on the outside were enormous, tattooed and bald gorillas with diamond earrings. The one in the middle was slighter and shorter. I recognised him immediately from his many appearances in the media. I was standing as a suppliant before Oleg Seratov himself.

He can only wish me harm, I thought to myself, *but will he spare the children?*

He eventually broke the silence. "You look uncannily like your twin sister. I sat opposite her in court for so many days."

At that moment his mobile telephone rang and he fished it out of his pocket. He listened intently and spoke a few unintelligible words, presumably in Russian. He put away his phone and gradually a broad smile spread across his face. He now looked far more attractive and much less menacing.

"I was waiting for that call," he continued. "Bronia, my soon-to-be ex-wife, has just been arrested by the British police and charged with the murders of your sister, her husband and Sasha Rubinski, as well as arson, fraud and money laundering. Bail has been refused as she is considered a flight risk. She will not trouble either of us again for many years, I think. She has far more important things on her mind now."

I did not know what to say. I still thought that we were in great danger. Oleg himself had plenty of reasons to silence me permanently.

"I'm sorry about your sister," he went on. "She didn't deserve such a fate, still less her husband. Sasha was a different matter. He was a soldier and knew he was playing with fire."

I plucked up the courage to interrupt him. "What are you going to do with us? Please at least spare the children. They are completely innocent of anything."

There was a long silence, which he eventually broke.

"You are all free to go. I have never had any quarrel with you. You can keep the Condor money. It is small recompense for the lives of your sister and her husband. There is nothing now to stop you returning to London and of course giving evidence against Bronia. Naturally, I will expect you to maintain complete silence in respect of any matters which could possibly relate to or embarrass me. My men will watch over you. In fact, here is the card of a lawyer I use in London." He produced from another pocket a standard if rather grubby business card. "Contact him as soon as you get back and make sure that you follow his instructions to the letter. He will see that my interests are fully protected."

I felt that those words contained a double meaning. On the one hand I was being taken care of but on the other I was being watched in case I stepped out of line, in which case the consequences could be terminal. I knew that my silence was being bought but I felt that the price was fair. I could see how Oleg was accustomed to operating. He could give generously but he always wanted something in return.

"Perhaps you would like to know how you were discovered. You did an excellent job of disappearing until you made one mistake. Both Bronia and I had access to all passport information and flight details. When you flew from Munich to Pisa, you put Bronia on the scent. It was only a question of time before she found you. It was even easier for me as I had another double agent in her office. Bronia was always mean and did not pay her people enough. I paid them twice as much. As soon as I heard that you had been found, I flew out to Grosseto in my private jet to join my men. They were never more than two hours behind Bronia's. I wanted to be there at the end."

I was still reeling at the revelation of all the double-dealing and duplicity when Oleg continued.

"I must tell you about my number-one spy in Bronia's office. You once spoke to her on the phone when you were trying to get through to Bronia. She listened in to your conversation with her. What you said was your death warrant so far as Bronia was concerned. On my instructions, my spy went to the police and told them the whole story so far as it incriminated my wife. She is now the principal witness for the prosecution and is in the British witness protection programme."

I didn't know what to say. I managed a strangled "Thank you" as he looked at his watch and turned away. He had finished with us for the moment and was giving orders to his men in Russian. One of them was nursing a bandaged and bloodied hand. Another had his right arm in an improvised sling. Others were now coming out of the house carrying large body-sized bundles wrapped in black plastic sheeting. There were five in all. I knew that they were the corpses of Bronia's men. I tried to shield the children from seeing the bundles but without much success. I could now see that the front door had been blackened by the explosion and was hanging off its hinges. Oleg saw where I was looking.

"Don't worry. My men will repair all the damage before they leave. I must go now."

At that moment one of those three-wheeled Piaggios, used by the local peasants to transport anything and everything and now driven by another of Oleg's men, chugged slowly into the square. The five plastic-coated bundles were dumped unceremoniously into its rear and it disappeared equally slowly down the hill. Oleg left with some of his men and without another word. The rest were deployed to show their building, carpentry and decorating skills.

I inspected the house and saw how much damage had been done. The floors were covered with pools of drying blood and cartridge cases everywhere. The walls were blackened and pockmarked with bullets, while the back door was in splinters. The men found pots of paint and brushes that I did not know we had. In an astonishingly short time, they had restored the house to its original condition, with the exception of the glass in the back door. I told them not to worry about it as I would get Mauro, our builder, to replace it the next day. At that, with beaming smiles, they each shook hands with me, embraced the children and vanished down the hill. I was left to ponder how men can be savage killers one moment and behave like benign uncles the next.

I was still in a state of shock with two frightened and bewildered children. I had no doubt that we were free to go back to London and that the heat was off. We would be safe there. However, I felt in no hurry to exchange the relative peace and quiet of Italian village life for whatever London had to offer. While our lease had another six months to run, I had inserted a break clause which I could exercise in two weeks' time. I knew that the arrest would be all over the English papers and would cause a sensation. It might provide a reason for my precipitate flight to the more perceptive lawyers in my firm in Ealing, as well as some kind of explanation for my sudden resignation from my City partnership.

We looked in a mirror and saw how filthy and bedraggled we were. I filled the large Jacuzzi bath with hot water and did my best to make all three of us look as presentable as possible. By now the wind had returned and driven away the cloud. The visibility was back to normal. We were ravenously hungry. Rodolfo's trattoria would still be open, so we went down the hill. I expected comments to be made about the strangers who had invaded the village and all the noise and activity that had taken place. I even asked Rodolfo in a disingenuous way whether anything unusual had happened that day.

He looked at me in silence for a long moment and paused before replying. "No, nothing out of the ordinary." But his words were accompanied by an unmistakable and slow wink. He, and no doubt others as well, had been paid generously to maintain a strict silence about the goings-on at the top of the hill. I knew that, if I probed further, I would get nowhere. Once again, Oleg's money had been well spent. In any event, the low cloud had fortunately concealed everything. For my part, I needed to make no explanations at all.

With no threats to face in London, I decided that we had to go back. I told Enrico that we were handing back the keys and the house in perfect condition. There was absolutely no evidence of the pitched battle that had taken place. Incidentally, I wondered how and where Oleg had disposed of the five neatly wrapped corpses but I thought it best not to dwell on the matter. I would never find the answer for sure. There was a deep freshwater lake some miles away where the well-weighted bodies would provide ample food for the fish and the swimming tourists would be unaware of their unsavoury companions. The locals considered the lake to be haunted and stayed away from it. They could have good reason now.

I arranged flights for us from Pisa to Gatwick and to terminate the open lease of our hire car. It was now a question of saying our farewells in the village. These were surprisingly painful. The children had made so many close friends at school and were loved by their teachers. Rodolfo and his wife, Nada, presented us with an enormous package of food and drink as though they feared that we faced starvation on the journey back to London. Eventually, we were off and this time I had no reason to look behind me to see if we had hostile eyes watching us.

25

There's No Place
Like Home

Sophie

It was raining as usual at Gatwick. As we had no home to go to, we checked into the Sofitel there for the night. The next morning, I rented a car and drove the children to their school. I was not sure how we would be welcomed after our precipitate flight but I need not have worried. Everybody knew about the arrest of Bronia, the murders and the arson attack. The children went back to their classes and were celebrities just for the time being. I went to see what had happened to the house. There was a fenced-off, blackened and empty site covered with piles of ash and soot where it had stood. The incendiary bomb had done its work well. Nothing was left standing. I realised that but for lucky timing and the warning from Hannah's spirit, we would not have survived the blaze and uttered a small prayer of thanks. I made a mental note to put in an insurance claim when I was settled with an office. The house would have to be rebuilt and the contents replaced but that was for another day. I was sure we would never wish to live there again but would sell it.

My next call was to the Ealing office. Once again, I was welcomed and had little explaining to do. Virtually everything that had happened to us was in the public domain. I was delighted to find how well the lawyers had coped in my absence. They had formed themselves into an informal cooperative and run the firm successfully. They had not known if or when I was going to return, so were always ready to hand back control to me at any time. I told them that I was not yet prepared to make any decision as I was uncertain at this stage about my own future. I resolved inwardly that if I went back to my partnership in the City, I would let them have the firm very cheaply. They deserved it for doing such a good job of running it in my absence and frankly we did not need the money any more.

I went to an estate agent and rented a furnished flat in Richmond. It would have to do for the moment until we became more settled. My lovely Topolino had been incinerated along with the house and Igor's old VW estate was languishing somewhere in a Heathrow car park, probably falling to pieces by now. I reckoned that the long-term car parks at airports contained many abandoned vehicles that could tell interesting stories. We needed a new car, so I went out and bought a Lexus SUV. The children were very excited when I picked them up from school in it and also when they saw the new flat. We spent the rest of the day shopping for necessities. I phoned Claudia on her mobile which she had replaced; she had retained her original number and I asked her if she would come back to work for us. She was delighted that we were safe and home. She was only temping at the moment and was very happy to take on her job as our housekeeper once again.

I took out the card that Oleg had given me and found myself talking to a very senior and distinguished partner in one of our main rival firms in the City. Only the very best was good enough for Oleg, even if what was involved was the cover-up of some very shady business, even violent deaths. It was agreed that I would liaise very closely with him and allow him to vet the draft of any statement I made before I submitted it to the police. He assured me that he and his staff were available to me at any time of the day or night. If I ever doubted it before, I now knew that limitless wealth buys the best possible professional services. I explained to him as subtly as possible that I shared his interest in making sure that his client was not involved in any proceedings to come.

I had been putting off the difficult call to Bill Ramsden. I had always been decisive in my dealings with the firm but now I could not make up my mind what I wanted to do. He too was delighted to hear from me and surprised me by suggesting we meet for dinner that evening. Until now, he had always been scrupulous about keeping our relationship on a strictly business footing. Extreme political correctness ruled all dealings between the sexes in our firm. I supposed that as I no longer worked for him, our relationship was now on a different level. I accepted gladly. I had always liked Bill and appreciated his championing of my cause over so many years.

Bill Ramsden

I surprised myself at how pleased I was to hear from Sophie. I had missed her. I was having a brute of a day and could not have fitted her in for an appointment in office hours anyway. The idea of meeting for dinner came to me in a flash. To hell with the risk of sexual harassment accusations, office protocols and all that jazz. Anyway, Sophie was currently not on the payroll so the rules did not apply in the same way. We agreed to meet at a quiet restaurant at the bottom of Chancery Lane. I was really looking forward to seeing her and the rest of the day seemed to drag by so slowly until it was time for us to meet.

Sophie

Claudia could babysit and I found I had just about enough in the way of decent clothes to make myself presentable for our encounter. On the way into town, I was trying to think of the last time that I had gone out with a man in this type of situation. I gave up the attempt. My life had for so long been unconventional. There were the years of non-stop work spiced with regular bouts of commercial sex and since Hannah's death I had been celibate, first of all totally involving myself in work at the Ealing office and the care of the children and then in keeping us all alive on the run. It was as though I had lost a large chunk of my normal life. I was feeling a bit like an excited young girl on her first date and told myself not to be so silly. Ours was only a business relationship anyway.

Bill Ramsden

Sophie looked terrific. She positively glowed. I realised how much I had missed having her around. At the same time, I thought how we had taken each other for granted working together, just like the filing cabinets. Sophie looked better than any filing cabinet. Of course I had read everything in the papers about Bronia Seratov's arrest, the alleged murders and the firebomb attack but I wanted to hear it all from Sophie and all that had happened to her since she left England. It was an amazing story. I marvelled at the effrontery of this Russian woman who thought she could come to London and behave like some savage beast in the jungle. It looked as if she was getting her comeuppance. I was also full of admiration for Sophie's resourcefulness in keeping herself and the children out of trouble for such a long time with the odds stacked so heavily against her.

I then started asking Sophie about her life generally. I was almost ashamed how little I knew about her. We had worked so closely together but we were virtually strangers – such is the culture of the big City law firm where work production is everything and the normal intercourse of life is forgotten. Of course I knew that she had had an identical twin sister who had also been a lawyer. She explained to me about their closeness and at the same time their need to live separate lives. I felt that a part of Sophie had died with Hannah and we both became quite emotional as we discussed it.

Sophie

I told Bill all about me. It should not have been necessary after all these years working together but the pressures of City life seem to make strangers out of colleagues. It was then my turn to find out about him. He too had suffered a great tragedy. His wife of eleven years had died of breast cancer two years ago, leaving him to bring up a nine-year-old son, Joshua. Bill still lived in their large, rambling house in Kew and was doing his best to be a good father, with the help of a series of inadequate housekeepers, while juggling his work commitments. He asked me what my plans were for the future. Did I want to come back to my partnership with the firm? I told him that it was still too soon for me to make up my mind. He was very understanding and said that the decision could wait so far as the firm was concerned. There was always a place for me if I wanted it.

At that moment, the waiter came over unsolicited with our bill. He explained that all the other customers had long left and the staff were ready to close and go home. I looked around, and sure enough the other tables were completely empty with the chairs stacked on them. We had been so absorbed in each other that we had not noticed how late it was. I offered to share the cost but Bill insisted on paying.

He had his car parked nearby and offered me a lift home. After all, we were virtually neighbours. His car was new and had that smell of leather that reminded me of an important incident in my life that took place so many years ago. After my seeming addiction to paid sex and complete control over my lovers, I never thought that I would be attracted normally to a man again but I felt very drawn to Bill. When we drew up outside my flat, it seemed the most normal thing in the world for him to turn towards me and embrace me. I could have offered him my cheek but our mouths somehow met and it was delightful. Neither of us wanted to prolong it, natural though it felt to do so. We were both very damaged and needed more time to recover.

"Can we do this again very soon?" Bill asked.

"Yes, but next time it's my treat," I replied.

26

Steppin' Out with My Baby

Sophie

I spent the day being interviewed by the police. I was careful to steer away from the subject of Oleg and Olga. After all, he was my benefactor and her death could continue to be treated as an accident. They were quite attentive to my theories, especially in relation to linkages. They concentrated on the firebombing. I had to be careful about the final battle in Italy but they were less interested in it as it happened off shore and there were enough lurid events within their jurisdiction to keep them happy. They agreed that, taking the easy option, because of my profession and the minor role I played in the matter, I could go away and draft my statement to submit to them.

I typed it up quickly and emailed a copy to Oleg's lawyer. His response, with a few minor alterations and corrections, came back equally rapidly. The police were much slower but they eventually had my signed statement in their possession. Oleg's name did not appear anywhere in it. They mentioned that the principal witness for the prosecution had been placed in the witness protection programme. I knew that they were talking about yet another of Bronia's employees who had been subverted by the offer of more money from Oleg. It was strange to be on the other side and giving a statement rather than taking one.

I felt very tired after the interview and it was a pleasure to be home, helping the children with their homework. Their English was not nearly as good as it had been when we began our precipitate flight. By contrast, their Italian was excellent for their respective ages. If I played it right, I would have two bilingual children to look after. I wondered if I could find an English/Italian school to send them to when the time came for their secondary education and meanwhile they needed tuition in Italian to keep it up to standard.

Bill Ramsden

I was impatient to see Sophie again. I was finding it difficult to concentrate at work. I took her to a Vietnamese restaurant in Hammersmith, which was a favourite of mine. The evening was even better than the last.

When I drove her home, I made sure I parked away from the street lights. We kissed in the car like teenagers. For the first time since Emma's death I felt sexually excited. I sensed that Sophie was feeling very much the same. I always fancied myself as a bit of a cook and I wanted Sophie to meet Joshua, so I invited her home to dinner on Saturday evening.

I was used to throwing meals together in not much time but I spent endless hours on this one, to the point that Joshua commented that it was shortening the time for our football practice. Joshua and Sophie got on very well together. She seemed naturally to be on his wavelength. We put him to bed and then sat down in candlelight to my carefully prepared meal. I liked the fact that Sophie had a good appetite. She had brought a great bottle of

Italian red wine as a gift. She made appreciative comments about the food but best of all was that she cleared her plate and even had a second helping of the dessert.

Afterwards, we sat on the couch in front of the fire, ostensibly watching television but in fact, with great pleasure, exploring each other's bodies. But for the sleeping presence of Joshua upstairs, I think we might have consummated our relationship there and then.

Sophie

I bought a very expensive bottle of Brunello di Montalcino for our dinner at Bill's house. He had gone to a great deal of trouble. The place was filled with flowers. I liked Joshua: he was nicely natural and unspoilt. In no way did he seem to resent my presence. Bearing in mind the recent and tragic loss of his mother, it would not have been surprising if he had been difficult with me but he was extremely open and articulate. The meal was absolutely delicious. Bill would not let me help with clearing away or loading the dishwasher and we were in a very mellow and relaxed mood as we sat in front of a blazing fire. We were much too interested in each other to watch the rubbish on television. I was completely ready for him and I could feel that he was for me but it wasn't the time and place with Joshua asleep upstairs. We were both building up a head of sexual steam.

A few evenings later, it was my turn to host Bill. He seemed to get on quite well with Charlotte and Ivan. I had to say that I was having visions of all three children under one roof, in one family.

The next day Charlotte took me to one side, almost as one woman to another. "I like Bill but is he really good enough for you?"

I swallowed hard but did my best to reassure her that I thought he was.

"If you say so, OK," she conceded.

161

Ivan was far more difficult. "I don't want a new daddy. I still love the old one."

I assured him that Bill would never replace Igor but he was not convinced. What gradually clinched it over a period of time was that Bill coached and managed the under-seven team of the Kew Super Kings in the local soccer league on Kew Green. There was a vacancy for a striker in the side. Although well underage, Ivan filled the role very successfully. A pugnacious, mobile, wiry redhead who could score goals with either foot as well as with his head was just what the team needed.

Either Bill or I had to take the plunge as abstinence was getting too much for both of us. After all, we were both mature adults and had no need to hold back or for a long courtship. I decided not to be a shrinking violet. I phoned Bill at his office on Monday morning to say that I had booked a midweek break in a rather fine hotel near Oxford and hoped that he would join me. He replied that nothing would keep him away. I almost had a mini orgasm on the spot in anticipation.

The hotel was perfect. I lost my 'virginity' to the most passionate, sensitive and caring lover that any woman could desire. We made love, slept, walked in the grounds, talked, ate and drank in a constant haze of delight for twenty-four hours. This was the midweek break to top all midweek breaks. We nearly stayed for another night but we both had pressing responsibilities for the next day.

Bill Ramsden

Sophie was wonderful. Before I met Emma, I was very much the man about town and sampled plenty of women, but this was completely different. I knew that I wanted to spend the rest of my life with her. Getting down on one knee and proposing seemed faintly ridiculous but I did it all the same. We were packed and ready to leave, so I caught her by surprise.

There was a long pause and I thought I had blown it. Then she suddenly threw her arms around me and shrieked, "Yes!"

Although we had a lot planned in London for the next day, this called for an extension of our stay. We phoned down and luckily the room was free. We just had to have an anticipatory honeymoon. We then spent the next hour on our mobiles, rearranging our and others' schedules. We could not keep our news from the hotel. The staff were all delighted and we enjoyed champagne on the house with the Michelin, much-starred tasting menu that evening.

Over a glass of vintage port, I turned to Sophie and said, "You realise that this makes one decision for you. Firm rules do not allow husbands and wives to work as partners. You'd better tell them that you're going back to work in your Ealing practice if you want to continue to keep me in the style to which I have become accustomed."

Sophie

That weekend we moved out of our furnished flat into Bill's house. There were separate bedrooms for all the children, who seemed to get on well enough together. It was time for Charlotte and Ivan each to have his and her own space. If anything, Kew was more convenient for their school than Richmond. However, we agreed that this house was a temporary measure only and in due course we would pool our resources to buy something else. Claudia took over as housekeeper and Bill fired the unsatisfactory incumbent.

The next day I went into the Ealing office, unsure how my news would be received. I need not have worried. They were delighted that I was coming back. We agreed to reconstitute the firm with us all as equal partners. I would be the senior partner, first among equals and take on the corporate and commercial work as well as the management. The less frantic pace of a suburban office gave me more time and energy for our three children and the new man in my life.

We had a simple wedding in the local registry office with one flower girl and two pageboys. I very much missed having Hannah at my side to share my happiness. Bill understood and said that he felt her approving presence. I did too.

Did I tell Bill all about my colourful previous sex life? Yes and no. A little bit of mystery goes a long way in a relationship, I think. Certain things are best kept hidden behind the closed bedroom door. He knew I was no virgin but I spared him the details. Ours is a reciprocal relationship and I neither required nor received a detailed list of his previous conquests. Our life together is about the present and the future. We can forget much of the past.

Another area where I had to tread carefully with Bill related to the involvement of Oleg in what had gone on. At first, I kept Oleg's name out of the version that I told Bill but he was much too shrewd not to spot the gaps in it. On balance, I felt it far safer to tell him the whole story despite any undertakings of confidentiality that I had given to Oleg's solicitor in London. I knew that I could rely on Bill to keep silent and not telling him everything about my dealings with Oleg was actually beginning to cause a rift between us. He was reading far more into my relations with the super-oligarch and actually becoming jealous. We needed to present a united front to the world in this potentially tricky area.

After a six-week trial, prolonged by the verbose speeches of the most fashionable QCs that Bronia could hire, the jury convicted her on three counts of murder, attempted murder, arson, fraud and money laundering. The judge gave her three life sentences to run concurrently as well as other bits and pieces. I was called as a witness in relation to the firebombing only. My evidence was relatively unimportant and my cross-examination was light. I appeared early in the trial and had the pleasure of reading the daily summaries of the case in the newspapers until the very satisfactory final verdicts. Up to that point, there were always a couple of heavies stationed at either end of our road whom I understood to be our protection provided by Oleg. I now expected them to disappear but their presence continued. Clearly Oleg was taking no chances in looking after us.

Our City firm gave Bill and me a wonderful wedding present consisting of a set of the most exquisite china including everything we could possibly need for twelve people for breakfast, lunch, dinner and tea. Perhaps this was a hint that they were hoping to be invited, as indeed some later were. I, of course, had lost all my goods and chattels and Hannah's too in the fire. Bill had a lot but it was all rather well used and chipped, so it was a very welcome gift.

A great surprise was a gift of an engraved silver samovar with an accompanying tray and six silver cups. The attached card was printed with the words *With the compliments of Mr and Mrs Oleg Seratov.* I knew from the gossip columns that the Mrs Seratov in question was Bronia's replacement. The phrase *Silence is golden*, written on the bottom of the card in handwriting I did not recognise, was easy to explain. There was no present from the previous Mrs Seratov. I'm sure she was much too busy adjusting to her new surroundings to think of us. There was quite a crowd outside the registry office and I am fairly sure that I caught sight of Oleg with two of his men at the back of it. He just wanted to make certain that Bill did the right thing by me. Not many people have a leading Russian oligarch as their personal guardian angel!

Hannah's Apparition

You would expect Sophie's little sister to have the last word. Since my death, I've appeared twice already but this time it's different. Before, I was either urging Sophie to take a terrible risk or warning her of dreadful danger. This time, I am content or as content as any mother can be when she is prevented from looking after her own children. I can rest easy now.

Sophie thought I didn't know how she used to take her pleasures on Sunday nights. We were both highly sexed and, while I had Igor in the early days especially and later Sasha to keep me happy, Sophie needed her satisfaction from men too. I may not have known the details but my twin's intuition got the general picture. It was unhealthy overall and she risked catching something nasty.

I always hoped that a good man would come into her life and I know that Bill is one of the best. It was ironic that my high-flying sister should end up running my suburban practice but what a good job she is making of it. I would have loved to bring up Charlotte and Ivan myself but it was not to be. If I could not do it, then Sophie is the next best person and she is doing a wonderful job in my place and I thoroughly approve of the children calling her 'Mum'. I like the fact that they now have a new big brother in Joshua, too. It would have been great for Sophie and Bill to have more children but I know that she feels that she has left it too late, even though that is not biologically the case. Anyway, she has her hands full already with three children, a loving husband and a full-time job!

Bronia got what she deserved. She was an evil woman. Oleg speedily divorced her and paid her nothing. There's not too much she can do about it while stuck in jail for life and she doesn't need money there anyway. If she tries to come after Sophie and the children, Oleg and his men are there to protect them. It would have been nice if the criminals who carried out Bronia's orders had been jailed as well. I'm pretty sure that at least some of them perished in the battle in Italy. Anyway, that type of man tends to have a short shelf life.

It's very sad that Igor got killed. He knew nothing about what was going on, though he did try to warn me off with regard to Bronia but I would not listen. It was his bad luck to be in the wrong place at the wrong time. He was a very good father. With the benefit of hindsight, we never should have married but what do you know when you're young and looking for love? He was not a bad man, but we were just unsuited and growing more so by the day.

Oleg was the fortunate one, but I feel that he makes or buys his own luck. He escaped punishment on this occasion. He's bad but not all bad like Bronia. He watched over and saved Sophie and the children and *then continued to look after them. For that alone I would forgive him anything.*

As to my own life and its violent end, it was just rotten luck but I played with fire and got burned. I can go now. I am content. There's nothing more to keep me here. I won't be coming back.